Scent of death

Bolan wormed his way across the pavement, taking special care, his nostrils flaring at the mingled scents of burning cordite, rubber, gasoline and human flesh. It was a smell that he had learned to live with overseas, and sometimes he imagined that it emanated from his pores when he broke a sweat.

Death's own perfume. The heady fragrance Bolan knew as *eau de combat*.

A blast of double-ought from Bolan's launcher sent the riot-gunner spinning like a dervish, crimson spouting from perhaps two dozen wounds. His partner may have seen it but, if so, it didn't slow him down. Once set in motion, he was bound to carry out the grim charade to its conclusion, do or die.

A short, precision burst from Bolan's M-16 decided that it would be "die" this time. The pistolero seemed to stumble over something, pitching over on his face and firing one last round into the pavement as he fell.

The Executioner scanned the bloody landscape: nine down, six to go.

MACK BOLAN®

The Executioner

DON PENDLETON'S
THE EXECUTIONER®
FEATURING MACK BOLAN®

FATAL ERROR

A GOLD EAGLE BOOK FROM
WORLDWIDE®

TORONTO · NEW YORK · LONDON · PARIS
AMSTERDAM · STOCKHOLM · HAMBURG
ATHENS · MILAN · TOKYO · SYDNEY

First edition October 1990

ISBN 0-373-61142-0

Special thanks and acknowledgment to
Mike Newton for his contribution to this work.

Printed in U.S.A.

A man that studieth revenge keeps his own wounds green, which otherwise would heal and do well.

—Francis Bacon

Revenge proves its own executioner.

—English proverb

My war is not about revenge, per se, but I remember how the payback game is played. If someone wants to take their hurt out on the people that I care about, they'll have to go through me.

—Mack Bolan

THE
MACK BOLAN®
LEGEND

Nothing less than a war could have fashioned the destiny of the man called Mack Bolan. Bolan earned the Executioner title in the jungle hell of Vietnam.

But this soldier also wore another name—Sergeant Mercy. He was so tagged because of the compassion he showed to wounded comrades-in-arms and Vietnamese civilians.

Mack Bolan's second tour of duty ended prematurely when he was given emergency leave to return home and bury his family, victims of the Mob. Then he declared a one-man war against the Mafia.

He confronted the Families head-on from coast to coast, and soon a hope of victory began to appear. But Bolan had broken society's every rule. That same society started gunning for this elusive warrior—to no avail.

So Bolan was offered amnesty to work within the system against terrorism. This time, as an employee of Uncle Sam, Bolan became Colonel John Phoenix. With a command center at Stony Man Farm in Virginia, he and his new allies—Able Team and Phoenix Force—waged relentless war on a new adversary: the KGB.

But when his one true love, April Rose, died at the hands of the Soviet terror machine, Bolan severed all ties with Establishment authority.

Now, after a lengthy lone-wolf struggle and much soul-searching, the Executioner has agreed to enter an "arm's-length" alliance with his government once more, reserving the right to pursue personal missions in his Everlasting War.

PROLOGUE

It had been a toss-up for a while, and some would question whether he was living, even now. For his part Vince Carboni had no doubts. There was direction in his life, a guiding purpose, and the background of his pain was necessary. The fire, so long ago, had placed a new perspective on his life.

It would make his ultimate revenge that much more pleasant in the end. Yes.

Approaching Sheridan, Wyoming, from the south, he followed Highway 90 with the dark mass of the Big Horn Mountains on his left. This close to the Montana border, the night was cool, but Carboni had his window down and the vents open on the dash.

He shied away from excess heat these days.

His destination was a stylish ranch house half a mile outside of town. No streetlights this far out. The dry runs had prepared him with a place to stash the car within an easy walk of where his targets lay asleep.

Before he left the car, Vince checked his gear. The Ruger .22 with a silencer attached had ten rounds in the magazine, a live one in the chamber. Latex gloves eliminated any risk of fingerprints, the right-hand one clipped and taped to compensate for missing digits, lost in the searing flames. In his pockets extra magazines, the penlight and his other tools were evenly distributed.

All set.

He didn't lock the car. The risk of meeting other prowlers out here was less than zero, and he would not have the luxury of time for fumbling with keys on his return. A moment saved could make the crucial difference between a smooth escape and something from the Keystone Kops.

He had no trouble with the fence—a simple clip job on the wire—and five more minutes brought him to the house. No dogs in residence, as he had verified on practice runs.

The front door was a bit exposed for Vince's taste. No traffic on the road so far, but you could never tell. In back, the sliding doors were locked, but he defeated the precaution with a simple lift that raised the left one from its runners, granting silent access to the house.

Inside, he took his time and let the penlight guide him through the unfamiliar rooms. A family room with fireplace, easy chairs and sofa, portraits on the walls. A homey smell of pipe tobacco. In the kitchen sharp knives were gleaming in a rack beside the stove. A spacious hallway leading to the bedrooms and the bath.

The sound of footsteps froze Carboni in his tracks. It was a sleepy, shuffling kind of noise, but he would not allow himself to be deceived. A hunter with experience in stalking human prey, he moved along the corridor on tiptoe, following the Ruger, hesitating as the open bathroom door spilled light across the corridor in front of him.

It made no sense to wait. Whichever one of them it was, he had to play the cards as they were dealt. He gripped the Ruger in his left hand, steadied with the pincers of his right and made his move.

The man was tousle-haired from sleep, his eyes half-closed as he reached down to flush the toilet. He became frozen in suspended animation as a stranger stepped across the threshold, gun in hand.

Carboni wasted no time on a greeting. One shot drilled his target's knee, the hollowpoint exploding into cartilage and bone. Before the scream could surface, number two was on its way toward impact with the shoulder socket, spinning Sleepyhead around and dumping him inside the shower stall.

It was enough. Carboni doubled back to find the master bedroom, flicking on the lights as he approached the bed. The woman blinked at him, confused, recoiling when she saw the pistol in his hand.

Recoiling, likewise, from his face.

He stripped the sheets and blankets back, his weapon forcing her to reconsider rash escape plans.

"On your face," he snapped.

"Where's Jack? My husband?"

"On your face!"

The lobster claw whipped out and stung her cheek before she grudgingly obeyed. He cuffed one arm behind her, then the other, tightening the ratchets to a point where she would have no play. Hooking thumb and index finger through the chain, he dragged her backward off the bed and dumped her on the floor. Despite the flannel nightgown—cut for comfort and nearly shapeless—he could feel the stir of passion as she huddled at his feet.

"Get up."

She hesitated, and he helped her, burying his pincers in her hair. Carboni found her handbag on the dresser, dumped it out and rummaged through its contents to retrieve a tube of lipstick. Biting off the cap, he used the lipstick as a crayon, writing one short word across the mirror.

Inch-high capitals in shocking pink. It couldn't miss.

"Let's go."

"My husband—"

"Will be fine, unless you piss me off."

Carboni didn't think the man would die. It would be simpler if he lived to make a phone call, but the matter was of no supreme importance either way. If all else failed, Carboni would be pleased to make the call himself.

Outside, the ground was cold and rough beneath the woman's feet. Carboni heard her sharp intake of breath as something jabbed her naked sole. Tough shit. It was a minor inconvenience in the scheme of things. He knew from personal experience that simple bruises were the very least of mankind's worries.

People lived with worse misfortunes, worse discomforts, every day.

And some, God bless 'em, died.

1

The load came in on Highway 40 from Saskatchewan, complete with escort. Seven hundred pounds of uncut China-white had been concealed in hidey-holes throughout the bodywork and chassis of a vintage Lincoln registered in Champaign, Illinois. The owners had presumably enjoyed a brief Canadian vacation, and it was nobody's business but their own if they opted to take the long way home, beginning with a pit stop in the tiny town of Noonan, North Dakota.

It was rather like a scene from Prohibition, Bolan thought. The priceless shipment rolling south with scout cars fore and aft to handle any problems. Handing off to stateside buyers in a rural spot few had ever heard of prior to checking out the map for perfect drops. A cash-and-carry trade-off on the windswept plains, with no one in the field of law enforcement any wiser. Fortunes piling up all around.

Not this time, Bolan told himself.

This time the Executioner was tossing in some unexpected stage directions of his own.

It was supposed to be a trouble-free delivery with representatives of Ernie Cathcart's tough Toronto syndicate delivering the goods—which they had probably purchased from the Chinese Triads—to selected representatives of Carmine Gagliardo's Kansas City family. The cash, it had been rumored, took a couple of suitcases to pack—and that had been in hundred-dollar bills.

The choice of Noonan for the drop had been inspired. They didn't exactly roll up the sidewalks at ten o'clock, but it hardly mattered. Everyone would be in bed by then, the solitary constable included, and his legal jurisdiction ended at the limits of the town in any case. There was a part-time sheriff's deputy assigned to handle any problems in the county's jurisdiction, but he hadn't been forewarned about the largest single criminal event in Noonan's history.

The Executioner was banking on surprise, and that meant pulling off the strike alone.

On Bolan's left the tubes of three LAW rockets lay side by side, a tarp beneath them. He had already pulled the safety pins to extend the telescoping tubes, and they were ready. All he had to do was pick one up and aim it, then press the lever that would send an armor-piercing high-explosive rocket on its way toward crunching impact.

On his right the tarp was anchored by an M-16 assault rifle, complete with an M-203 40 mm grenade launcher mounted under the barrel. Extra magazines and ammunition for the over-under combo ringed his waist, with the Desert Eagle .44 Magnum revolver riding Bolan's hip in military leather. Tucked beneath his arm, the sleek Beretta 93-R waited in reserve.

And waiting was the key.

His targets had arranged the meet for twelve-fifteen, by which time Noonan's single traffic light was blinking yellow, north-to-south, and flashing red along the east-to-west two-lane road that intersected Highway 40. To play things extra safe, the meet wasn't scheduled to take place in Noonan proper, but precisely three-point-seven miles due north, where some benighted whiz kid from the county planning board had dropped a picnic area and rest stop. There were public washrooms and a pay phone, tables with their legs securely anchored in concrete—and there was privacy.

It really was the perfect drop, except for one small problem.

No one on the planning end had reckoned on a visit from the Executioner.

In a few more moments Bolan meant to thank them personally for the oversight.

The Kansas City buyers had arrived at midnight, cruising past to check the drop for stakeouts, doubling back to take a closer look when nothing major caught their eye. They checked the rest rooms, even used a flashlight underneath the picnic tables in a search for microphones, but no one thought to take a stroll around the dark perimeter.

Not that it would have mattered. Bolan was prepared to take them out on the spot. In a pinch he reckoned he could meet the shipment on his own and wreak the necessary havoc, even if his careful plans were somewhat altered in the process.

But no change of plans proved necessary. Satisfied with their inspection of the site, the city boys had settled down to wait, secure in having done their job according to the book.

While Bolan, crouching in the darkness, had already thrown the book away.

The northern team arrived with headlights blazing, trusting in the Kansas City boys to deal with any problems at the drop, and Bolan saw them coming from a mile away. The Lincoln's point car was an old Camaro with a lot of power underneath the hood and four beefy gunners crowding the interior. The backup was a Chevy four-door, ditto on the passengers, with space in back to bear the Lincoln's driver home again.

Nine guns, plus six already waiting at the drop.

Mack Bolan liked the odds.

He waited for the new arrivals to unload, but two men kept their seats in each one of the escort cars. The driver and a shotgun rider, just in case. That made it simple. Close to one-third of the hostile force eliminated in a single stroke.

If he could pull it off.

Lifting one of the LAW rockets to his shoulder, Bolan sighted on the Canadian point car, fixing his sights dead center on the driver's door. The weapon was designed to kill a tank or other armored vehicle at ranges up to five hundred yards, and Bolan had shaved that distance by something like ninety percent for the present operation. Even if they had the sleek Camaro reinforced like Al Capone's old touring car, it wouldn't count for squat.

He ran the doomsday numbers down in backward order, squeezing off on zero, and the second tube was on his shoulder by the time his first projectile reached its target. Sudden thunder rocked the picnic area, and an oily fireball gobbled up the point car and its occupants before they had a chance to realize that they were marked for death. The windows' pebbled safety glass, blown outward by the blast, reflected ruby firelight like a thousand marbles scattered on the pavement.

Two down, and that left Bolan with thirteen hostile guns to go.

The driver of the tail car tried to save it, but he stalled his engine with an overzealous foot on the accelerator. Seven seconds into Armageddon, Bolan sighted on the Chevy's windshield and squeezed off, the rocket trailing fire en route to its collision with the bull's-eye.

This detonation seemed to mash the target vehicle as if a giant boot had crushed it from above. The occupants had no more than a millisecond to review their lives before they were incinerated, and the fuel tank kicked in with a secondary blast that fused the Chevrolet into a twisted heap of scrap iron.

Scrubbing four, and that left ten, plus the driver of the load itself.

The Lincoln's driver was on foot, consulting with the money men, when hell broke loose around him. Bolan took the time to use his final rocket on the limo, anyway, to guarantee that none of the Toronto shipment would survive to reach the streets. He sighted on the trunk in profile, aiming low to catch the gas tank perfectly, and let her fly.

It was a gratifying light show, flaming streamers arching through the night, but some of the surviving gunners had finally spotted him. The last rocket's trail had pointed back to Bolan like a long, accusatory finger etched in fire, and scattered rounds were snapping overhead as he retrieved the

M-16, preparing to advance and finish off what he had started.

Just to keep them guessing, Bolan shifted to his left, along the roadside gully and emerged some thirty yards from his original position. In their panic no one seemed to notice, and he cut the gap in half before one gunner—singed and shaken by the fiery thunderclaps—picked out his silhouette against the background of the night.

"He's over he—"

The M-203 launcher cut him off with a storm of finned fléchette rounds, turning him to sushi where he stood and peppering the Kansas City car with tidy holes.

Advancing, Bolan thumbed a high-explosive round into the launcher's breech and stroked the trigger one more time. The sole surviving vehicle erupted into smoke and flame before him, with a lake of burning gasoline from ruptured fuel lines spreading swiftly underneath.

A member of the home team burst from cover, slapping at the flames that licked around his calves and ankles and were climbing toward his groin. The M-16 coughed out a 3-round burst, and he was history, a smoking rag doll stretched out on the pavement, deathly still.

Guided by the muzzle-flash, the others had Bolan's number, and they were weighing in with handguns, plus a pair of automatic weapons. Bolan hit a fighting crouch and scuttled to his left, allowing them to fire at shadows for a moment.

Nine guns, and any one of them could do the job if Bolan allowed himself the killer luxury of overconfidence.

He fed the launcher with a buckshot round and blasted through the ring of fire without a special target. Anything to keep them down while he advanced to killing range.

The smokescreen worked both ways, and he had shaved the distance down to forty feet when one of the defenders made his move on Bolan's right. The guy was fast, and it was obvious that he had practiced with his Ingram MAC-10 submachine gun to control the little monster's cataclysmic rate of fire. Instead of rattling off his load in a second and a half of pyrotechnic glory, he preferred to nurse it, tapping out three rounds at Bolan, followed by another three or four and so on, gaining ground.

The Executioner went belly down and let his automatic rifle do the talking. At a range of fifteen yards, the 5.56 mm tumblers dumped his human target in an awkward sprawl, spread-eagled, while his Ingram skittered out of reach across the blacktop.

Seven hostiles down and eight to go.

He wormed his way across the pavement, taking special care, his nostrils flaring at the mingled smells of burning cordite, rubber, gasoline and human flesh. It was an odor that he had learned to live with overseas, and sometimes he imagined that it emanated from his pores in place of normal body odor when he broke into a sweat.

Death's own perfume. The heady fragrance Bolan knew as Eau de Combat.

The next two made it easy, figuring that no one could defeat a pincer movement executed with sufficient zeal. One of them had a stubby shotgun, and the other fired a pair of automatics as he ran, unloading with the sort of what-the-hell enthusiasm taught by Hollywood films. Looking good was what mattered, and the heroic try was enough for survival.

Wrong again.

The riot-gunner caught a blast of double-ought from Bolan's launcher, and the impact set him spinning like a dervish, crimson spouting from perhaps two dozen wounds. If his partner had seen, it hadn't slowed him down. Once set in motion, he was bound to carry out the grim charade to its conclusion—do or die.

A short, precision burst from Bolan's M-16 decided that it would be "die" this time. The *pistolero* seemed to stumble over something, pitching over on his face and firing one last round into the pavement as he fell.

That left six.

He wondered if the flames were visible in Noonan or if there was anyone abroad to see them at that hour of the night. The last thing Bolan needed was a troop of volunteer firefighters blundering into the midst of the action with half a dozen enemies still primed to fire on anything that moved.

He kept on moving, seeking targets, and the other side obliged. Two gunners opened up on him with side arms, popping out from cover to seek their target and ducking back behind the Lincoln after one or two quick rounds. He caught the taller of them with a knee-high burst that dropped him into Bolan's line of fire, the tumblers ripping through him like a chain saw as he fell.

The dead man's partner dropped from sight, and Bolan thumbed a high-explosive round into the rocket launcher, shifting slightly to achieve the proper angle for his shot. It was impossible to pinpoint his assailant, so he dropped the HE can behind the Lincoln, trusting shrapnel and the shock wave to complete his work. He was rewarded with a scream, immediately stifled as the blast propelled his adversary headlong into the inferno of the burning car.

Four left.

A flurry of activity on Bolan's flank alerted him to danger, and he turned to face another Ingram artist, tracking right to left and firing as he ran. The gunner seemed preoccupied with looking out for number one, but Bolan couldn't trust him to keep running once he reached the shelter of the dark perimeter. An active shooter on his heels was one thing Bolan didn't need.

He tracked the runner, leading slightly with the M-16 while parabellum rounds carved divots in the blacktop to his left. A steady burst, sustained for maximum effect, and contact punched the target through a sloppy pirouette, depositing his body on the nearest picnic table.

Bolan dropped the rifle's empty magazine and fed a fresh one into the receiver, counting down the odds as he resumed the hunt. He could have disengaged and let them go—the heroin and cash had been his major targets—but it ran against the grain to leave a job unfinished and the savages at large.

He caught a glimpse of shadows breaking for the men's room, crashing through the swinging door, but his attention was distracted by another figure moving toward him through the smoke, making no attempt to hide.

The gunner's suit was torn and grimy and there was an ugly gash across his forehead, but his hands were steady on the 12-gauge shotgun that he carried. He was jacking in a round when Bolan saw him, and their guns went off together, the shotgun blast against the rapid crackling of the M-16.

One pellet traced a line of fire across the soldier's bicep and another burned inside his thigh. The blacksuit acquired smears of crimson to its color scheme, but Bolan won the toss. A rising zigzag burst decapitated his opponent where he stood.

A rapid scan of the perimeter by firelight, then he turned his full attention to the men's room. It was constructed of cinder blocks and painted a utilitarian tan color. The metal door was operated by pneumatics and designed to close by itself. The two surviving gunners might be anywhere inside, prepared to open fire the moment he stepped across the threshold.

Two explosive rounds remained for Bolan's launcher, and he used them both to clear the way. His first charge blew the door completely off its hinges, nearly folding it in half and driving it across the room to strike the farthest wall with a tremendous clang. His second round struck home before the echoes died away from number one, exploding when it struck a urinal and spraying shards of porcelain around the room. As Bolan entered, ruptured pipes were spewing water toward the ceiling like geysers gone berserk.

One of his targets lay beneath the sinks, a fist-sized portion of his skull sheared off by flying shrapnel from the double blasts. Ignoring him, the soldier moved to a position where his M-16 could cover the three toilet stalls at once.

A scuffling sound from the middle stall betrayed his quarry. The guy had tried an age-old trick by crouching on the toilet seat, but nerves and the concussion of the high-explosive charges had destroyed his sense of balance. Bolan watched one foot scrape briefly on the floor, retreating, dropping back again, before he shook his head and held the automatic rifle's trigger down.

He didn't know who occupied the stall—it might have been a simple flunky or the leader of the pack—but it didn't matter either way. He emptied out the magazine in one long burst, beginning with a figure 8 that knocked his target off the stool and dumped him in a corner, finishing with half a dozen rounds for an untidy coup de grace.

He left the reek of ruptured bowels and cordite in his wake as he retreated, jogging through the darkness to the place where he had parked his Bronco, hidden from the road. He took the time to check his wounds and found them superficial, nothing that some iodine and Band-Aids wouldn't fix.

No sirens came from Noonan yet as he stowed his gear and followed Highway 40 south through town. On Highway 5 he motored east through Larson, past Columbus, braking outside Flaxton for an all-night truck stop with a phone booth planted in the parking lot.

His call to Washington was routed through a string of cut outs, ticking off the best part of a minute while he waited, static lisping in his ear. It was a new procedure, and he was relieved when Hal Brognola's voice came on the line.

"What's shaking?"

"It's a wrap," the Executioner replied. "Are we experimenting with a party line these days?"

"I'm airborne—or, I should say, *we* are. Leo's back there sawing logs."

"That's Leo. What's the rumble?"

"It's a little touchy for the phone," Brognola said. "If you can swing it, I'd appreciate a face-to-face."

A small alarm bell started clanging in the back of Bolan's mind, but he ignored it. Worry was a premature down payment on disaster.

"Where and when?"

"I'm thinking Rapid City."

"South Dakota?"

"Right. How far is that from where you are?"

"I'd have to check the map. Let's say three hundred fifty miles."

"It's on your way to Denver, though."

The soldier frowned. "It would be, sure, if I was going."

"We can talk about that when I see you," Hal replied. "I'm flying into Ellsworth Air Force Base, and we've got bookings at the Travelodge on Fairmont. Can you meet us there?"

"No problem. It should take me six or seven hours."

"Fair enough. You'd better get yourself some coffee for the road. And, hey—good job with Gagliardo's cowboys."

"Right."

The line went dead, and Bolan cradled the receiver, frowning. Rapid City? *Denver?* What the hell . . . ?

He knew that it would take a special case to drag Brognola out of Washington, with Leo Turrin at his side, to fly all night for a connection at a Travelodge in South Dakota.

Something major, then, and Bolan didn't have a clue what it might be.

He put the problem out of mind and fetched a thermos bottle from the Bronco, counting on the truck stop for the kind of coffee that would light a fire inside him and compel him to remain awake for six or seven hours on the road.

A nagging hunch told Bolan that his mission wasn't finished, after all.

In fact he thought it might be just beginning.

2

Bolan picked up Highway 85 in Williams County, north of Williston, and pushed the Bronco south through brooding darkness at an average speed of eighty miles per hour, slowing as he passed through prairie towns with not a sign of life. He met no black-and-whites along the way, a stroke of luck, and sunrise caught him outside Sturgis, South Dakota, twenty minutes from his destination. Picking out the Travelodge was easy, and he dropped a quarter in a pay phone two blocks down, connecting with Brognola long enough to get the number of his room.

"You made good time," Hal said in greeting after they had shaken hands. "I guess you're beat."

"Not really."

He had marched or driven through the night on more than one occasion, sometimes going days without a wink of sleep in combat situations. Five straight hours on the road was nothing.

"Hey, Sarge."

Leo Turrin pumped his hand and offered coffee, tea or something stronger.

"Coffee's fine," said Bolan as he settled into a standard motel chair and let himself unwind. "What's happening?"

"Before we start," Hal said, "why don't you fill us in on Noonan."

There was nothing special to report, and Bolan ran it down in generalities, using the antiseptic jargon of the battlefield. He didn't bother with a body count, but let Hal know that the cash and heroin had both gone up in smoke.

"That should hold Kansas City for a while," Brognola said when Bolan finished speaking. "I don't like to run these operations back-to-back, but we've got something rotten going down in Denver, and it seems you may have one foot in the door already."

"Oh?"

"You've seen the file on Niccolo Armato?"

"He's the man in Denver," Bolan said, recalling mug shots of the mobster who had come up through the ranks in southern California to finally secure a fiefdom of his own.

"He *was*. These days he's got some competition from Chicago. Seems Armato's making such a mint on pharmaceuticals that Don Pagano's got the urge to wet his beak. He's got Patsy Scimone and a troop of hardmen in Denver right now, sniffing around and hoping Armato jumps the wrong way."

"That sounds like Bureau business, Hal."

"It would be, normally...but as it happens, there's already been some contact."

"Oh?"

"A couple of Scimone's buttons bit the big one Monday night, and Patsy's in a snit. The trouble is, he's not sure who to blame."

"Why's that?"

"They found a marksman's medal with the bodies."

Bolan's eyes went hard. It wouldn't be the first time that a mobster with a score to settle tried to hide behind the Executioner. At one time, while his war against the Mafia was in full swing, the phony Bolan strike had been a favorite tactic of the Eastern families. It started going out of style when one or two practitioners got caught and had to face the wrath of *La Commissione*.

"Armato's playing games?"

"It's not that simple," Hal replied. "There's something happening in Denver that we haven't put our finger on as yet. It looks like someone wants you on the scene."

"What makes you think so?"

"Well..." Frowning, Brognola glanced at Turrin, then his eyes came back to Bolan's face. "It's Val."

He felt the short hairs rising on his nape and understood that any news he got from this point on could only be the worst.

"You knew she lived in Sheridan?"

"Wyoming, right?"

"Somebody dropped in night before last, uninvited. Jack stopped two rounds, in the shoulder and the knee. He'll be all right, if you don't count the plastic kneecap and a limp for life. Whoever staged the hit—Jack saw only one man—took Val with him. We've had nothing in the way of ransom demands since then, but he took time to leave a note. One word in lipstick on the bedroom mirror—'Denver.'"

A rush of memories had carried Bolan miles and years away. He pictured Val Querente as she looked the night they met, wrapped up in terry cloth and calling for her cat outside a smallish house in Pittsfield, Massachusetts. Bolan had been running from the Mob and the police, a bullet in his flesh and fresh blood soaking through his blacksuit. She had saved his life that night, no questions asked, and in the days to come Val nursed him back to fighting strength, her sympathy becoming something else along the way.

Their mutual attraction, blooming into love, had taken warrior Bolan by surprise. He wasn't ready for commitments at the time—indeed, he had no prospect of surviving that first contest with the Mafia—but he could no more turn his back on Valentina than he could decide to give up breathing. By the time he left her sanctuary for the killing grounds, their lives were joined in every way that counted, short of matrimony, and the warrior knew that home and family had slipped beyond his reach forever.

It was Val's idea for her to shelter Johnny Bolan at a time when every contract killer in the country hoped to earn himself a million tax-free bucks by wiping out the remnants of the Bolan family, root and branch. The Mob had reached them once, in Boston, but the Executioner had won them back with fire and thunder on a scale unprecedented in his one-man war. The locals still swapped tales about the day the Executioner had come to town.

When Bolan learned of Val's engagement to a federal agent on the Orgcrime Task Force, one Jack Gray, his first reaction was a feeling of relief. Despite the love that he would carry to his grave, he felt no pangs of jealousy. Val needed more than yellow clippings in a scrapbook—she *deserved* more—and her new life offered Johnny the stability of an adoptive home. The Executioner had long since made his peace with the realities of love and war, accommodating loneliness as an accepted part of the experience. And it always helped to know that she was contented. But if they hurt her...

It all flashed through his mind within perhaps a second, and the warrior said, "I see."

Brognola's forehead seemed permanently creased, and again he glanced at Turrin before his eyes came back to Bolan. "It's a trap, of course."

"A sucker play," said Leo, sounding gloomy.

"So?"

"We'd like to know what's going on...but I can't ask you to participate when they're already dusting off the welcome mat."

"You haven't asked. I'm volunteering."

As Brognola knew he would. It was a game they played from time to time, but at the moment Bolan had no patience with the rules.

"I might as well be honest with you, guy. We haven't got a clue who's holding Val. It could be either team."

"You're betting on Armato," Bolan said. It didn't come out sounding like a question.

"Well..."

"Why not? Scimone's men are taking hits, and someone's leaving medals as a blind. What better way to back it up than for Armato's men to put me on the scene by any means available?"

Brognola shrugged. "I won't deny it's crossed my mind, but don't count out Chicago when it comes to double-dealing. Hell, for all we know, Scimone could have put his own boys on the spot to make it look like Nicky's dealing with the Executioner. If the Commission buys it, its the kiss of death, for damn sure."

Bolan thought about it for a moment, turning puzzle pieces over in his mind. "Did Jack describe the shooter?"

"It was pretty vague. He's standing in the bathroom, half-asleep, when Mr. X drops in and plugs him twice. The guy was all in black, he used a .22 with a suppressor and we're pretty sure he had some facial scars."

"What kind of scars?"

"Like skin grafts. Tight and shiny, anyway. That's really all Jack saw before things started popping and he wound up facedown in the shower."

"So, I'm looking for the Phantom of the Opera?"

"I've been thinking it may have been a mask," said Turrin. "With the way things happened and the state that Jack was in, he can't be sure exactly what he saw."

"It's all we've got," Brognola said. "The Bureau keeps an index of tattoos and scars, that kind of thing, but so far nothing in the mug files rings a bell with Jack. We're blowing smoke."

"Assuming that it's not a mask, you may not have the guy on file."

"It's possible, of course. Unlikely, though, if he's affiliated with the Families as a shooter."

"We're assuming that," said Bolan. "On the other hand, suppose he was a wild card."

"That would mean he knows about the Denver action," Hal replied. "The locals haven't leaked a word about the marksman's medals yet."

"And it would also mean," Leo said, "that he's bucking you along with the Chicago Family. With odds like that, he'd have to be a raving lunatic."

"Like me, you mean?"

"Well, now—"

"I haven't seen enough to pass on anybody's state of mind," said Bolan. "I'm just looking at the options."

"Sure. Okay."

"You said that Val was taken night before last."

"Right." Brognola cleared his throat and gave his tie a restless tug. "We didn't want to call you in until—"

"I finished off the Kansas City job?"

"Goddamn it, no! Until we ran down every lead ourselves."

Bolan instantly regretted the unworthy thought. "Sorry, Hal."

Brognola waved it off. "You know how much Val means to me. To all of us. *I* know how much she means to *you*. You think I'd piss her life away to make a lousy score?"

"I know you wouldn't."

"Jesus in a jumpsuit, we've been turning over every rock that we could think of. First I thought it might be linked to something Jack had done while he was with the task force— chickens coming home to roost, that kind of thing—but a shooter with a grudge would never leave his target breathing while he took off with the wife. Of course the 'Denver' clinched it, but we still don't have a thing to go on, namewise."

"Someone did his homework," Bolan said. "My link with Val goes back a ways, and linking her with Jack is something else." A sudden thought intruded on the warrior's mind, and it was reflected on his face.

"Don't worry," Leo said. "We ran a quiet check on Johnny, and he's fine. We'll keep a shadow on him for a while, until we wrap this up."

"Does he know why?"

"There wasn't any way to keep it from him," Hal replied. "He's got a kind of bond with Jack and Val, you know. It's not like blood, exactly, but—"

"I know. It's what I wanted for him."

"Anyway, you know the kid. He wants a piece of this the same way you do."

Bolan's mind rebelled. "No way! I don't care if you have to lock him up, Hal. Keep him clear of this. I mean it."

"Do I *look* stupid? Are my pants on backward here or something? Christ, you think I'd turn him loose on this when it appears that someone's got a fix on your relationship with Val already?"

"I don't want him anywhere within a hundred miles of Denver," Bolan said.

"Agreed. He's sitting tight with Jack for now, and I've got people with him all the time. We've had some words, for what it's worth. I think he understands that he'd be in the way on this one. He remembers Boston, incidentally."

"We all remember Boston, Hal. I never counted on a replay."

"Well—"

"I can't make any promises for Denver," Bolan said.

"I didn't ask for any."

"Val comes first, no matter what I have to do. I don't want anybody in my way."

"We can't exactly call the locals off a gang war in the making."

"Let them take their chances, then. I'll do whatever's necessary to secure Val's release. If she's been damaged..."

Silence hung between them for a moment. Each of them remembered Boston, and Bolan's closest friends on earth had seen the Executioner in kamikaze mode. They knew that risk meant nothing to him when a loved one's life was on the line.

"If you need anything—"

"I've got your number," Bolan said.

"I'm thinking maybe I should spend a couple days in Denver," Hal replied. "Soak up some sun and try to catch a handle on the action with Armato and Scimone. It couldn't hurt."

"I don't want any baby-sitters."

"Me?" Brognola grinned. "I've been behind a frigging desk too long."

It was an overstatement, Bolan knew. The man from Washington could still go one-on-one with damn near any adversary he could name, and if Brognola's fists were insufficient for the job, he had a marksman's eye.

Right now, the big Fed's eyes were dark with anger and frustration, the desire to help...and something else. The last time Bolan could remember seeing Hal look quite that way had been when *his* wife and children had been hostages. The Executioner had been of some assistance then, and Bolan didn't need a crystal ball to know that Hal was eager to repay the karmic debt in kind.

"You don't owe me a thing," he said.

"That's bullshit," snapped Brognola, "and it doesn't have a thing to do with why I'm staying. We don't need a Mob war in the Rockies at the moment, and we definitely don't need Don Pagano's family taking over any new preserves. I still get paid to roust this scum, in case it slipped your mind."

"No interference?" Bolan pressed.

"It never crossed my mind. If anything, my being there may help to clear the way. At least the Bureau boys won't try to hang you up."

The plan made sense, but Bolan still had reservations. If it blew up in his face and he was forced to make a sacrifice, he didn't want Brognola stepping in to queer the play for friendship's sake.

"You know," Brognola said, "I hate to say it, but we don't have anything to prove that Val's alive, so far. Without a contact, we can't even ask for proof that she's all right."

"I thought of that," said Bolan. "Either way, I've got a score to settle. Val's condition won't affect the deal. It only sets the price."

"Okay. I didn't want you building up your hopes...in case."

"It's been a long time since I hoped for anything," said Bolan.

But in truth he had not given up on hope. In one respect it was the essence of his war—the hope that somehow, someday, savage man would be eliminated as a threat to civilized society.

It was more dream than hope, and since he knew that dreams do not come true, the price of Bolan's fantasy was everlasting war against the savages. He paused to rest from time to time, but there was always some new adversary, some new struggle, waiting when he punched the clock.

The war had not begun with Bolan, and it would continue after he was gone. That much, at least, was guaranteed. But while he lived, he would continue making every moment count against his enemies. Because he could.

One man *could* make a difference.

One man *had*.

One man was not prepared to stand by on the sidelines, watching while barbarians ran roughshod over all the decent men and women of the world. It was a challenge Bolan had accepted in his youth, and once the battle had been joined, there was no honorable way to disengage.

No way to turn against a friend.

"I may need something in the way of ordnance," Bolan said at last.

Hal brightened. "Name it. I'm a little short on howitzers and nukes right now, but if we're talking small arms, I suspect that I can throw some things together."

Bolan's smile was weary to the bone. "I want to get a feeling for the local action first. If I come up with any special needs, I'll let you have a shopping list."

"Okay," Brognola said. "We've got two rooms booked through tonight, in case you want some sleep."

"I'll do my snoozing on the other end. Time's wasting."

"Right."

They shook hands all around, and Bolan made the proper noises as they wished him luck. From that point on, he knew that planning, nerve and pure audacity would have to serve. He left his enemies to count on luck.

They were about to find that it had gone sour.

3

Who can pinpoint the moment when a grand obsession first takes root and starts to grow? Who marks the point in time and space where simple dedication alters like a changeling to become insanity?

For Vince Carboni it had started on a hunting trip to Oregon. No simple expedition, to be sure. He was by profession a contract killer for the Mafia. Much more than that—he was a member of the underworld elite, a bearer of the dreaded Black Ace death card.

And his prey in Oregon had been a human being.

More specifically the object of his hunt had been Mack Bolan.

No small task, considering the badass warrior's record of evasion and retaliation. No one in the head shed kept a body count these days—too damn embarrassing, for one thing—but Carboni's research told him that in his one-man war the Executioner had killed *no less* than fifteen hundred men, from lowly soldiers to the highest-ranking members of the Mafia Commission. The final number may have been a good deal higher, but the fifteen hundred helped to put his target in perspective.

Research.

For Carboni it was half the battle on a major operation. He had never been a cowboy, satisfied to hit and run like some two-bit beginner when he had an opportunity to do a job in style. With Bolan, where so many other guns had tried and failed, he simply had no choice.

So Vince had done his homework. Starting with the day that Bolan first sucked wind in Pittsfield, through his school days and enlistment in the Army, double tour in Vietnam, the summons home to bury members of his family and seek revenge against the local family he blamed for their demise.

It should have ended there, of course, if anyone in Pittsfield really had their shit together, but the local team had fumbled every ball that came their way, and Bolan wound up kicking ass across the board. Carboni gave the bastard credit, but it hadn't been quite the one-man show that everybody thought it was.

There was a woman in the background, and Carboni learned her name. Querente, first name Valentina, had been Pittsfield born and raised. A looker, from her photographs. The kind of girl you might take home to mother, in a pinch. She had nursed Mack Bolan and then became his lover. When the badass warrior split from Pittsfield, she had taken charge of baby brother, raising him as if he was her own.

The syndicate had tracked them down one time, when she enrolled young Johnny Bolan in a Massachusetts private school that boasted Harold Sicilia's brat among the members of its student body. It had been a careless move, and Harold the Skipper took advantage, bagging both the woman and the boy to bait a trap for Bolan. Mack the Bastard took the bait, all right, but after swallowing the hook and line he also took the pole. And then he swallowed Harold the Skipper, chewed him up and spit the stupid bastard out along with more than half his Boston soldiers. Val Querente and the boy had disappeared before Carboni caught their scent, and they were nowhere to be found.

But research pays.

When Bolan slipped away from him in Oregon, Carboni knew that it was not the end. His reputation was at stake, his very standing in the brotherhood, and he was not about to let the matter rest while he was trailing in the numbers. Bolan had embarrassed him, and Bolan had to die. Case closed.

Before the gig in Baltimore, Carboni had consulted a psychiatrist and other so-called experts, scoping out a profile on the man he was determined to eliminate. Before he finished, Vincent felt he knew his target inside out, knew all the buttons he should push to call up a particular response.

And he knew Bolan's weakness. The guy was basically a sentimental fool.

When someone Bolan cared about was placed in jeopardy, he pulled out all the stops to save their bacon, or, if he arrived too late, to punish those responsible for any injury they might have suffered. Time and time again, the soldier placed himself at mortal risk to help a friend or ally, gaining strength from righteous anger once he settled down to whipping ass. It was a pattern that Carboni saw repeated in New York, in California, in New Jersey, in Detroit—around the world, in fact. The Executioner would no more leave a loved one hanging than he would enlist with *La Commissione*. It simply wasn't in him.

Theoretically, then, Harold the Skipper had been right in Boston. The fuck-up came when he applied his theory to the world of flesh and blood. And that, Carboni told himself, had been a case of personal incompetence.

Carboni didn't have a chance to try his scheme in Baltimore. There had been too much going on when he arrived, and by the time he got his action squared away, the shit was in the fan. Even so, he had come close to nailing Bolan.

Until the wind changed.

Thinking of the night he almost died made Vince Carboni's skin itch. But that was nothing new. There had been a horrible debt to pay for surviving the all-consuming flames. The brief but thorough downpour had taken him from the jaws of death and left him in hell. The pain came first, in combinations and varieties his mind had never contemplated, working on his ravaged nervous system day and night, around the clock. At first the docs tried heavy-duty morphine to relieve his suffering, convinced that he would die within a day or two in any case, but Vince had fooled them. He had pulled through, and by the time they realized they had a live one on their hands, he was addicted to the little hypodermic pick-me-ups.

That made it misery times two, recuperating from the burns that covered seventy-five percent of his body and kicking his addiction at the same time. It was a first for Vincent's doctors, though you wouldn't catch them saying that where anyone could hear. It made things . . . difficult.

When Vince Carboni tried—and even when he didn't—he could call up every moment of the burn ward therapy that saved his life. It hurt to simply lie in bed, but he was not allowed that luxury. The saline baths were torture, but the worst of it was when the nurses came to peel away his shriveled, damaged skin.

It happened every fucking day, like clockwork, and he ground his teeth until they loosened in his gums to keep from screaming. Smiling faces told him that the daily peel was a must to regenerate new tissue and prevent unnecessary scarring.

Right.

A glance in any mirror told Carboni they were blowing smoke. Plastic surgery had helped a little—he looked halfway human now, above the shoulders—but he could have gone out trick-or-treating anytime without a mask.

So much for modern medicine.

A dozen trips to different operating rooms had left him mobile, and it could have been a damn sight worse. The flames had somehow spared his feet, his genitals and buttocks, plus a portion of his lower back above the kidneys. He could get it up all right, but hookers charged him extra once they took a gander at the Halloween mask Vincent wore year-round.

Who needed romance, anyway?

Performance in his chosen field of expertise was something else, and doctors at the burn ward had assured him he would "probably" regain "about two-thirds" of his mobility if he was willing to accept a regimen of exercise and therapy. Carboni wasn't satisfied to gimp through life, a shadow of his former self, and if the skin grafts were beyond his power to control, Carboni had more latitude in plotting out his convalescence.

Starting from day one, he had begun to double the assignments from his therapist, ignoring jolts of pain that filled his eyes with tears. He punished wasted flesh with calisthenics, working overtime on weight machines and treadmills while his muscles screamed for mercy. On the day they cut him loose, the doc in charge told Vince he was amazing, and Carboni flashed a crooked, crinkled smile.

He didn't tell the doctor that a measure of his own determination to survive had been provided by the mental image of the man he meant to kill, the man responsible for months of wasted time and suffering—Mack Bolan.

Carboni needed Bolan dead because he'd been humiliated by the man on two occasions, then left for dead in Baltimore. He was familiar with the jokes that made the rounds among his so-called brothers, assholes giggling behind his back about how Bolan singed his ass in Baltimore and Vince came out a *real* "black ace." They cut the crap when he was in the room, but still it galled him and fed his notions of revenge.

And all the time, he kept a little list.

But first he had to get the man who made him what he was today.

Preparing for the rematch was a whole new game. For openers the surgeons had removed three fingers on his right hand that had fused together, and Vince was forced to practice firing different weapons with his left. It was the same for throwing knives and handling other tools, but he had put the lobster claw to use when he began a stiff refresher course in martial arts. Before he finished punching heavy bags and ramming both arms elbow-deep in barrels filled with sand, the ugly pincer had become a lethal weapon. One more small addition to his arsenal.

Of course, it wasn't easy picking up where Vince had left off. The ruling capos had their doubts about a near-death burn case carrying the death card, and he had to prove himself like some green rookie. Jobs were difficult to come by once the big boys saw how Vincent's scars would make him stand out in a crowd, but there was always someone waiting to be iced. Some wetback competition in Miami. A "protected" witness in L.A. An underboss whose ego had outgrown his common sense in Youngstown. Most of the Commission finally agreed Carboni was as good as new— for jobs where he could work at night or wear a mask.

And then he started talking Bolan.

He was moderate at first, reminding anyone who cared to listen how the guy had rubbed their nose in shit these many years. It wasn't bad enough that Bolan had a thing for the brotherhood; he had embarrassed and disfigured Vince Carboni in the bargain. How could *La Commissione* sit back and swallow crap like that when it was still within their power to reach out and punish Bolan for his sins?

The answers he received had been lukewarm at best. For most of the presiding capos, it appeared that Bolan out of sight was Bolan out of mind. They didn't want to use a hornet's nest for a piñata when their lives were running more or less on track. If Bolan started fucking with the brotherhood again, there would be ample opportunity to take him out—and they would use a proper team to do the job. No one-man armies need apply.

With time Carboni grew more strident, carping on his favorite theme until the doors began to swing shut in his face. By that time he was too far gone in this obsession to perceive that he was sewing seeds of doubt about his own professional reliability and turning former allies into enemies. Deprived of his perspective, Vincent never understood that he was driving the Commission to a point where members would be forced to judge him, with the choices boiling down to life or death.

The final vote was a formality. It didn't hurt to keep a few psychotics on the payroll, for those "special" jobs, but raving lunatics were dangerous to everyone around them. It just couldn't be predicted when one of them might spill his guts to strangers, and Carboni knew enough to bring the house down if he started telling tales.

So the Commission voted death. Unanimously. Vince was not informed of the decision, but a messenger was chosen to enlighten him.

The contract on his life had taken Vincent by surprise, but he recovered swiftly once the grapevine tipped him off. The shooter came for Vince expecting easy pickings, but it went down rather differently. One up, one down. Carboni was insulted by the quality of talent sent against him, and the treachery of his employers made him furious.

It was a revelation when he thought about it, and he understood why Bolan had been able to survive so long. Somewhere on *La Commissione*, the bastard had a friend—or more than one—who played the devil's advocate and fed him secret information, running interference with the brotherhood. The traitors recognized Carboni's genius, and he scared them shitless. They were out to kill him now, before he could destroy their agent in the field.

In his delusionary state, Vince never stopped to ask himself why any member of the ruling board would cast his lot with Mack the Bastard. It was obvious, and therefore, must be true. It didn't even matter who the traitors were, since every member of the board was compromised through acquiescence. *All* of them were guilty by association, and he planned to deal with each of them in turn, as time allowed.

When he was finished with the Executioner.

Carboni had resumed his homework from the moment that he left the burn ward, sniffing after Bolan through a maze of paperwork and dead-end leads to find the crucial information he required. A piece of living bait that would be simply irresistible.

He shaved the field to two—the brother and the woman—both of whom had disappeared. Carboni concentrated on the woman first, because he thought she would be easier to find and her discovery might give him two live wrigglers for the price of one.

In fact it wasn't easy and it wasn't cheap. The money posed no problem for Carboni, since he counted on the brotherhood to fund his private expedition. Cashing in his private knowledge of the way things work and who runs what, he dropped in on a pair of numbers bankers, a cocaine distributor, a major kiddie porn producer. Each of them was thrilled to help support his personal crusade; they couldn't hand the money over fast enough.

It was a shame Carboni had to pay them back in lead, but that was business, after all.

A dead man told no tales.

With cash in hand Carboni started buying crucial information. Anyone could find out whatever he needed these days if he was tough, persistent, and he had a wad of greenbacks thick enough to gag a goat. Someone, somewhere, had the answers—on computer disks, in dusty files or tucked away upstairs. You simply had to find the proper source and then apply the necessary leverage to produce results.

No sweat, except that tracking down a human needle in the haystack still took time.

An average of one hundred fifty thousand persons disappear in the United States each year. The ones who fade on purpose—as opposed to homicide and kidnap victims, plus the rare amnesia cases—often change their names to throw pursuers off their track. For women in America, a new identity could be acquired in three distinct and separate ways...but all of them left tracks.

A legal name change would require at least one trip to court with various petitions, depositions and what have you. That, in turn, would open files at federal, state and local levels, changing everything from drivers' licenses to listings with the IRS. Petitioners could have their records sealed in special circumstances—the Protected Witness Program was a case in point—but there was always *someone* with a key to that forbidden file drawer, and Carboni had his contacts where it counted.

That avenue yielded zilch.

A second means of vanishing, preferred by fugitives, eliminated courts and lawyers by relying on the artists of the underground. With cash in hand a vanishing American could pick up birth certificates and passports, a diploma or a driver's license—anything her little heart desired. The runner needed contacts, but they weren't that difficult to find, and when the paperwork was done, no messy records were left on file in Washington or at the county courthouse.

There were always memories, of course, and they were subject to the stimulation of a well-placed bribe or sharp blade. Carboni knew the best—and worst—of those who filled the public's need for off-the-record paperwork, and he had asked around from coast to coast.

Again, no dice.

And that left marriage.

It was perfect, when you thought about it. Say "I do," and no one gave a thought to questioning your motives. Changing names was standard operating procedure—unless the woman varied from the norm for feminism's sake—and it was over in a flash.

But there were still those files.

It took Carboni eighteen months to run his quarry down, and he was interrupted several times by shooters trying to collect the bounty *La Commissione* had posted on his head. As aggravating as they were, the interludes helped Vincent stay in shape.

The second hitter made his move in Boston while Carboni tried to pick up Val Querente's stone-cold trail. The man made the crucial error of attempting to surprise Carboni in his own hotel room, and the maid had something extra to clean up next morning when she came to make the bed and change the towels.

In Houston there were two of them, a stone-faced Mutt-and-Jeff routine. They had a bright idea involving a highway ambush, hoping that Carboni would be easy pickings in his car, but it takes skill to orchestrate a running gunfight, and they didn't make the grade. Carboni buried them near Galveston to keep their masters guessing for a while, and mentally added two more notches to his gun.

In Reno number five had used a hooker for his decoy, thinking Vince would be so grateful for a piece of ass that he'd forget the training of a lifetime. Wrong again. Carboni killed them both with pleasure, and he left their naked bodies in a clench that managed to divert police in the direction of a nonexistent jealous lover.

His persistence paid off three weeks later in Nevada, where a clerk unearthed the wedding license linking Val Querente with a civil servant named Jack Gray. Not *any* civil servant, mind you, but a federal agent, lately serving with a special Justice task force on the Mob. Gray's address led Carboni back to Massachusetts, on from there to Oklahoma City, and at last to Sheridan, Wyoming. In the process, he had managed to obtain adoption papers for a young man known as Johnny Gray, but he postponed that search until he checked the woman out.

And Sheridan, Wyoming, had paid off. In style.

Carboni had his bait now, and the killing ground had been selected with a fair amount of care. It was coincidence, of course, that Nick Armato and Chicago's shock troops were preparing for a rumble in the Rockies. Denver was convenient, and Carboni had been helping things along with input from the sidelines, taking out a couple of Scimone's third-stringers, leaving Bolan's mark behind to make things interesting. When Mack the Bastard came to town— as he inevitably would, to find his woman—he would find an army waiting for him on the streets.

And if he turned that army into hash, believing the Chicago Family had snatched his squeeze, so much the better. It would be a small down payment on the grief Carboni had in store for *La Commissione*. Vince frankly didn't care what happened to Armato or his other "comrades" in the brotherhood.

There would be grief enough to go around.

But he would have to keep a sharp eye out for Bolan nevertheless. It would not do if one of the Chicago cocks got lucky, picking off the big one for a million-dollar bounty on the side. When Bolan bought the farm, Carboni meant to be there, and he planned to close the sale himself.

He owed the bastard that much, anyway, for all that they had meant to one another.

And he owed it to himself.

Soon now, and he would know when Bolan hit the mile-high city by the shock waves his arrival caused. The bastard never did a job halfway, and when he hit the bricks in Denver, they would feel it all the way to Vegas and Los Angeles.

Mack Bolan was dependable that way.

He was the kind of guy that you could count on for a blast.

Carboni had a few ideas in that regard himself, and he was anxious for the chance to try them out.

Not long, he told himself.

Not long at all.

4

It was approaching one o'clock when Bolan entered Denver, rolling south on Highway 25 from Cheyenne. He had resisted the urge to detour through Sheridan, fighting an impulse to visit the scene of the crime. Jack Gray was in the best of hands, and anything that Bolan did on Val's behalf would have to be accomplished on the killing ground that lay in front of him.

Before Bolan left the Travelodge in Rapid City, Hal had filled him in on all the crucial details of the Denver set. He knew that Niccolo Armato had been sent to Colorado as a pointman for the southern California syndicate, renewing old connections and establishing new footholds in the Rockies. Aspen, Vail and other tourist traps ranked high among his targets, with Armato cultivating wealthy customers who lusted after different kinds of "snow." In Denver and environs, he ran dope and women, supervised some gambling operations and was said to dabble in pornography.

Armato's income had increased dramatically since he was transferred from Los Angeles, and life was sweet.

Until he caught a whiff of the Chicago stockyards in his own preserve.

The Windy City's capo, Don Giuseppe Pagano, was an avaricious man who never got enough of anything. At one point, in the thirties, it was rumored that he had been married twice without the benefit of a divorce. When word leaked out, he flipped a coin and thus became a widower, but gluttony remained a way of life for Don Pagano. Anything he wanted would be his in time, regardless of the cost or risk involved. And there were some within the brotherhood who said Pagano wanted *everything*.

Frustration can be galling for a would-be emperor. Pagano had begun his tenure in Chicago with a ritual of testing boundaries, pushing out in this and that direction till he met resistance, backing off with insincere apologies before a shooting war broke out. Within a span of three short years, New York and Philadelphia rebuffed him in the East; he ran afoul of Cleveland and Detroit along Lake Erie; Kansas City blocked him to the south with reinforcements from Miami and New Orleans. Chicago's appetite became a subject of debate among the members of the Mafia Commission, and Pagano was advised—with all respect—to mind his manners.

On the plus side of the ledger, there were still casinos in Las Vegas to be plundered, with investments in Atlantic City, the Bahamas and beyond. Pagano had connections with Colombians and Cubans, Corsicans and Chinese Triads—all of whom made certain that the Midwest junkie population never went without. It was reported that he owned a certain U.S. senator and merely had to lift a telephone receiver to produce results in Washington.

But there comes a time in every glutton's life when he rebels at wolfing down the same meal every day. Pagano hungered for a change of scene. New worlds to conquer, and his scouts reported that the Colorado Rockies were the place to be. Snow bunnies and celebrities. The all-night parties. Life-styles of the rich and decadent. An endless potpourri of sex and snorting. Let the good times roll.

The problem lay with Nick Armato and his L.A. backers. California mobsters looked at Denver and the rest of Colorado as their private happy hunting ground, and they were not amused by the suggestion that they ought to share. Much less that they should pack their bags and leave the whole damn state to Don Pagano as a gift. It went against the grain, and there were rumblings of dire retaliation if the new, unwelcome visitors did any more than ski and sun themselves.

Now, according to Brognola, fireworks had begun, and someone wanted Bolan in the middle of the action. Wanted him enough, in fact, to kidnap Val Querente and employ her as a piece of human bait.

Chicago's man in Denver was Patsy Scimone, a hard-core protégé of Don Pagano who had made his bones with double murder at the tender age of eighteen. He followed orders with the grim tenacity of a Gestapo agent, but he also had the nerve to improvise when Don Pagano gave him room to run. In Denver, backed by thirty guns, he had already done some poaching on Armato's turf, seducing or coercing several dealers into ordering their coke and skag from Illinois. It was a start, and Bolan knew that Nicky A. was never one to take an insult lying down.

But was Armato crazy-brave enough to try an end run with the Executioner? More to the point, if Nicky was behind the move, how had he tracked Val down?

The "how" had troubled Bolan from the moment when Brognola had broken the news, but he had been around the hellgrounds long enough to realize that no one in the world was perfectly secure. A president could always be assassinated. Fugitives could always be tracked down. Protected witnesses could be unearthed despite new faces, new identities. It was a simple law of nature in the world that Bolan occupied.

Instead of wasting time on how the enemy discovered Val, he concentrated on the problem of retrieving her from hostile hands. First up, he had to find out where she was and who was holding her.

At first glance the Armato team appeared to be the leading suspects with the most to gain. Scimone's force had lost two men already in a strike that Nicky A.—or someone else—was blaming on the Executioner. It stood to reason, then, that drawing Bolan in would help Armato to eliminate Scimone without appearing to involve himself in the hostilities. A classic case of misdirection, but the soldier wondered if it might not be *too* pat.

A second possibility, suggested at his Rapid City meeting with Brognola, was the Reichstag fire scenario. Assuming that Scimone—and Don Pagano—wanted Denver to themselves, it would be useful to initiate a war and cast themselves as hapless victims of an unprovoked attack. Scimone could easily afford to waste some button men, drop marksmen's medals at the scene and later claim that Nicky A. had struck a bargain with the Executioner. If he could make it stick, a Bolan link would damn the southern California family to exile from the brotherhood, and when the smoke cleared, Don Pagano might be nursing his cigars beside the blue Pacific, in the western outpost of his empire.

One more possibility, but nothing he could prove. To scope the action out and rescue Val, he needed solid information, and the warrior was prepared to kick some ass in its pursuit.

And it had to go down very soon.

Brognola had supplied a list of Rocky Mountain targets, and the Executioner decided to begin his razzle-dazzle with Armato. As the local warlord of the moment, he had most to gain from beating back Chicago's thrust at any cost, and Bolan made it sixty-forty that Armato would be slick enough for a diversionary play.

His destination was a supper club on Colorado Boulevard, two blocks from Denver's Celebrity Sports Center. Nicky A. owned the building, the land it sat on and the souls of the front men who covered his action. Not that the business was anything other than what it appeared. There was no gambling on the premises, no drugs, no prostitutes upstairs. They served a killer surf-and-turf, maintained a classic wine cellar, and Armato relied on the place to launder income from his less legitimate endeavors. In the afternoons, before the club was opened to receive the high-class dinner crowd, Armato's people sometimes used the private office as a counting house, secure from prying eyes and law enforcement microphones.

The lot was nearly empty when he parked his Bronco near the entrance, checking out the Lincoln and Mercedes standing side by side around in back. The older, less expensive vehicles would all belong to members of the staff. He made a mental note that he would need another car, together with a place to stash his gear, before the Denver blitz got underway for real.

The door was open, and he spent a moment in the foyer, waiting for his eyes to grow accustomed to the semidarkness. Scattered lights were burning in the dining room just to let a pair of janitors perform their duties, and the sound of muffled voices emanated from the kitchen.

"We ain't open, mister," one of the custodians informed him.

"I'm not buying," Bolan answered, slipping the Beretta from its armpit holster. "Where's the office?"

"Back th-that way. By the bar."

A slugger was emerging from the kitchen as he got there, took Bolan in with one quick glance and growled, "What the fuck?"

The 93-R clued him in as a parabellum mangler punched through his forehead with sufficient force to drive him backward through the swinging kitchen doors. A startled shout and clash of cookware heralded the dead man's entrance as he toppled to the floor.

A gilt-edged sign declared the office Private, but the Executioner was not in the mood to stand on ceremony. Sweeping through, he caught three men in shirtsleeves, hunched around a desk with stacks of currency and open ledgers jostling for space. The honcho was an overfed man in his forties, double chin above his collar, hairline creeping backward toward his crown. The bookends flanking him on either side were lean and mean, with hardware showing and rodent eyes that had no difficulty in identifying trouble.

Bolan gave them points for trying as they made their move, one shooter peeling off to either side, each digging for his piece in the hope that his companion would be first to draw the hostile fire. It was a case of either-or, and Bolan took the right-hand gunner first because he seemed a trifle quicker on his feet. No point in giving up the edge.

His first round struck the lanky gunner more or less dead center, painting crimson on his stylish shirt and spattering the wall behind him as it kept on going. Impact rocked the not-so-tough guy on his heels, and he collided with a filing cabinet on his short trip to the floor.

The shooter on his left was drawing from a crouch as Bolan spun to face him, squeezing off a rapid double-punch from fifteen feet away. The bullets rocked him on his haunches, and his gun hadn't cleared leather when the light winked out behind his eyes, the dead weight settling with a thump like dirty laundry dropping at the bottom of a chute.

That left the money man, long on sweat and short on combat training, but he wouldn't give it up without a fight. One pudgy hand was groping in the nearest drawer when Bolan shot him, taking time to drill a hot round through his shoulder joint. The big man's swivel chair rolled backward, stopping short when it collided with the wall. The sound that issued from his lips ranked somewhere in between a whimper and a scream.

The counter's hands were limp and empty as Mack Bolan moved around the desk. His eyes were focused on the pistol, waiting for another muzzle-flash to close his show, and Bolan had to slap him sharply on the cheek to break his trance.

When he was certain that he had the wounded man's attention, Bolan drew a marksman's medal from his pocket and dropped it on the desk.

"I'm here," he said. "Somebody knows why. Tell Nicky I'll be looking for him."

"Sure." A gleaming ray of hope showed in the dazed eyes. "I mean, yes, sir."

He found a briefcase on the floor and dumped its contents, scooping fifty thousand dollars off the littered desk.

"A little something down on what he owes me," Bolan said. "You won't be needing a receipt."

"No, sir."

"Let's hear the message."

"Someone knows why you're in town. Tell Nicky you'll be looking for him."

"Close enough."

Outside, he scanned the lot again and satisfied himself he had no audience for his retreat. The Bronco would be safe enough for one more job before he stashed it and acquired another set of wheels.

One down and one to go as Bolan laid the groundwork for his Rocky Mountain war.

HE DIDN'T MEAN for the Chicago troops to see him yet, and Bolan mapped his plans out on the short ten-minute drive to reach Scimone's command post in suburban Skyline. With a spin around the block to firm things up, he knew exactly what he had to do.

The target was a storefront office in a bankrupt shopping mall. The other six or seven shops had folded one by one, and the banners putting up the space for lease had been ripped down when Don Pagano's pointman bought the mall for cash. There was a chance Scimone could turn a profit on it in the future, but the empty buildings served him well enough right away. No traffic in the parking lot, a decent field of fire in the event of an attack, and Patsy's men could mob up in the other vacant shops if times got hard. In terms of keeping up a front, the mall was perfect. Don Pagano had his foothold—a legitimate investment, and it was small enough that Patsy could dismiss Armato's protests as a sign of creeping paranoia.

Best of all for Bolan's purposes, the shopping center had a vacant lot across the street.

He parked the Bronco, circled to the hatchback and retrieved his M-16, together with a belt of ammunition for the M-203 launcher. Bolan made the range at fifty yards, an easy shot for either rifle or grenades from his selected stand.

Outside the storefront office, half a dozen cars were lined up in adjacent slots. Three Cadillacs, a Jag, two smaller four-doors of domestic manufacture. The sun's glare on the plate-glass windows kept him from a head count, but he didn't really care how many gunners were inside the shop. Another moment and Chicago's shock troops would be in for one or two shocks of their own.

He fed the launcher with a high-explosive round and chose the first car on his left. A Caddy. At the present range he could have made the bull's-eye blind, and Bolan took his time to get it right. A clap of thunder, and the gas tank blew a heartbeat after the grenade, with oily smoke obscuring the battlefield in seconds.

He skipped one Caddy, leaving number two to catch alight from spreading pools of gasoline, and sighted in on number three. The detonation had shattered windows up and down the mall, and he could hear men shouting in the storefront office, trying to decide if they should rush out front to fight the fire or beat it out the back while there was time.

He helped them with another HE round and watched the jag disintegrate, its graceful outline twisted into something black and hopeless by the force of the explosion. Pieces of the engine and the bodywork were airborne, peppering the lot and buildings with a rain of shrapnel as the vehicle went to hell.

Round four took out the last car on his right and caught the other four-door in a sandwich, trapped between the Jaguar and its flaming look-alike. There was another secondary blast from somewhere in the middle of it all, and yet another, fuel tanks blowing as the fire took over and demanded room to breathe.

Behind the wall of smoke and flame, he saw stick figures milling helplessly about. The searing heat prevented them from doing anything constructive, and he made their minds up with the M-16, unloading one full magazine on automatic as they broke for cover, scrambling to save themselves. He hadn't meant to hit them, but if one or two went down, the Executioner wouldn't be losing any sleep.

He stowed the hardware quickly and, unseen, retreated under cover of the smoke. The wail of sirens overtook him three blocks from the scene, and Bolan curbed the Bronco as a line of fire trucks hurtled past him, with two patrol cars bringing up the rear.

He wished them luck.

The Executioner had made his presence known in Denver, but Scimone would be guessing when it came down to assigning blame—he would first look to Nick Armato as a potential suspect.

Fair enough.

It wouldn't hurt to have the opposition snapping hard at one another's heels while Bolan tried to name the players in this game of life and death. He had his money on the table, and by the time he finished dealing, someone would be looking at the dead man's hand.

5

The sun was going down as Bolan tooled his brand-new Volvo two-door through the streets of Lakewood, passing the Green Gables Country Club on his left. The car had been purchased with Mafia cash, depleting his afternoon's take by some thirty percent and knocking the socks off a local dealer. More cash had gone into the rent and cleaning deposit on a three-room apartment he might never use, but it was good to have a place on tap.

Armato's palace stood within an easy stone's throw of the country club, providing from its upstairs windows a panoramic view of the golfers hacking toward the thirteenth green. Armato might have played those links himself in more pacific times.

But he wouldn't be thinking sports just then. The L.A. underboss and acting chief in Denver had more pressing matters on his mind. Like standing off invaders from Chicago and, at least since half-past one that afternoon, discovering why Mack the Bastard was in Colorado.

Bolan intended to help him on the second point, but that meant contact, eye to eye. It was a risky move and might blow up in Bolan's face, but he was counting on the standard Mafia mentality to carry off his stratagem. Role camouflage should do the rest, at least he hoped.

The Volvo had been chosen in a compromise between utility and flash. The same was true of Bolan's suit, the shoes he wore, the mirrored aviator shades. He had an image to project, and a substantial part of it was attitude.

Armato's home was short on acreage, but it was still surrounded by a six-foot wall to give the occupant some privacy. The gate was tall wrought-iron, and two men were standing guard as Bolan pulled his Volvo up outside. One of them keyed a button, and the gate rolled back just far enough to let him through. His partner hit the switch again when the vehicle was clear and closed the gap.

"There something I can do for you?" the gate man asked. His eyes were taking Bolan in—the parts that he could see— and he had slipped the single button on his sport coat, bringing hidden hardware that much closer to his hand.

"I need to have a word with Nicky."

"Who?"

"Armato. What's the matter, don't you know who signs your paycheck?"

"I work for *Mr.* Armato," the gunner replied, angry color surging up from his collar to his hairline, reminding Bolan of a thermometer on overload. "He's not receiving visitors right now."

"That so? I think he's going to be very disappointed if I drive away."

"I guess I'd better take a look at some ID."

He palmed the playing card and passed it over. A magician's trick.

"The name's Omega," Bolan said. "If Nicky needs my pedigree, he'll have to call New York."

Staring at the ace of spades, the gate man had already lost his color. He recognized the death card of the brotherhood's elite Black Aces, and it was a shock to see the frigging thing in person. Years before, when he was still a punk kid skipping school and drawing light probation from the juvey judge, the Aces had been feared from coast to coast. They were the hard arm of the Mafia, invested with authority to waste a capo on their own initiative if they could justify the hit to *La Commissione*, post mortem. Lately, since the Bolan wars, there were supposed to be no more than half a dozen Aces still alive—some said they *all* went down—and rumor had it that it was never known who they were working for.

The gate man knew only two things. First up, he knew an Ace would kill with the same emotion normally reserved for swatting a mosquito, and the bastard would forget about the victim by the time you hit the ground. Second, he knew that there was no way in the world to make this call himself.

"I'll have to phone it in."

"You do that."

Bolan sat and watched the gate roll back two feet, the gate man slip inside, the gate clank shut again. The gunner disappeared inside a little guardhouse roughly twice the size of a phone booth, while his partner stayed in place and eyed the Volvo's driver with a mixed expression of concern and curiosity.

Two minutes later, when the gate rolled back, it kept on going, opening the way. The gate man he had spoken to returned with Bolan's card and passed it through the Volvo's open window.

"Hey, I'm really sorry if I came on strong," he said. "I had no way of knowing who you were."

"Forget it." Bolan gave the punk a winning smile. "You're paid to come on strong. That's why they picked a strong man for the job."

He drove on through before the gunner had a chance to thank him for the compliment, reflecting that it never hurt to win the buttons over when you had the chance. Downrange he might be forced to try some move inside Armato's camp, and the investment of a kind word now could pay off later when the chips were down.

The driveway looped around a wide expanse of manicured lawn, and there were shade trees spaced along the outer wall. As he approached Armato's house, he had a choice of veering right and parking in the front or following a narrow single lane around in back, where servants and deliveries would be received.

He parked in front and pocketed the keys, his eyes taking in the pair of hardmen waiting for him on the porch.

"You guys must be the welcome wagon."

"Right this way, sir."

"Anything you say."

The older man led him through the double doors, his sidekick falling in behind to close the box. Inside, the dominant motifs were leather, polished wood and money. Bolan's escort hesitated in the foyer, turned to face him, and he felt the young one breathing down his neck.

"I'm sorry, sir, but we've got orders to check everyone for heat."

"I'll save you all some time," he said. "I'm packing, and it stays with me."

"My orders are—"

"I understand your orders," Bolan interrupted, "and they make good sense, but no one ever counted on a situation quite like this. I'm here to do your boss a favor, maybe save his life, but I'm not playing any asshole games. The piece stays where it is. If that's not good enough, then I can walk away. Or you can try to take it, if you're tired."

"How's that?"

"Of living."

There was restless movement at his elbow, and Bolan swallowed down the urge to turn in that direction. "Tell your boy I hope he's reaching for suppositories," he said. "'Cause anything he pulls on me, I'm gonna have to shove it up his ass."

"Relax there, will ya, Billy?"

"Yeah, okay."

"I'll have to ask the man, you understand? He says no heat...." The house man spread his hands in a helpless gesture of surrender.

"Fair enough. His call."

They moved along a corridor with portraits on the wall and lavish carpet underfoot. Their destination was a tall oak door, where Bolan's escort knocked, received permission to proceed and disappeared inside. The warrior flashed a grin at Billy while they waited, and he saw the kid was trembling in his boots.

The older house man reappeared some thirty seconds later, putting on a crooked little smile.

"This way, sir."

Bolan shouldered past him, and the door snicked shut. He spent a moment scoping out the study—leather bindings color-coded on the built-in bookshelves, heavy drapes and chairs that must have weighed a ton. Then he fully faced his host.

"Omega, is it?"

"At the moment."

Bolan shook the offered hand. Armato's grasp was firm and dry, the rest of him well-groomed and tidy. Power was evident in Nicky's chest and shoulders, and dark suspicion hooded his eyes.

"Nobody told me you were coming."

"No one was supposed to."

"Have a seat, why don't you? Would you like a shot of something? Anything at all?"

"No, thanks. I haven't got a lot of time."

"Okay." Armato settled into a massive chair that seemed to swallow him alive. "What's on your mind?"

"I had a little free time on my hands," he told the mobster, "so I thought I might drop in and save your life."

"How's that again?"

"You're looking at a world of trouble, Nicky. This Scimone business . . . and the rest of it."

"I guess you'd better spell that out," Armato said.

"We're playing head games? Fine with me. Word is, Chicago's got a hunger for the action you've been building up these past few years. A certain capo and his bird dog like to throw their weight around, okay? They figure L.A.'s far enough that they can pull it off, and maybe no one else will mind."

"This capo just might lose himself a bird dog if he lets it off the leash," Armato said.

"No skin off me," the Executioner replied. "But he's got many other dogs—you follow? Kennel's full. He keeps them hungry so they don't ask lots of questions when he turns them loose.''

"This guy sounds like a lousy neighbor.''

"Some would say he makes himself a nuisance.''

"So?''

The Black Ace shrugged. "I'm only making conversation, but it could be that some other people wouldn't mind a new face in the neighborhood. They might be glad to see this problem handled by a man who knows his business.''

"Should I take it that the neighbors would be helping out with the elimination of this problem?''

"It's a possibility, but they're concerned about this business with the wild card.''

Uneasy now, Nicky shifted in his chair.

"Am I supposed to have the inside line on that?''

"I'm passing on what people say. They figure if it's your backyard, you ought to know who's playing in it. One guy says the wild card isn't even here. He figures *you* iced Patsy's buttons and you're setting up a straw man for the fall.''

"That one guy wouldn't be a certain capo from Chicago, I suppose?''

Another shrug. Very casual.

"It's not my job to carry tales and point the finger, understand? A friendly word, that's all.''

"Well, you can tell your friends the wild card's here, all right. He iced three boys of *mine* this afternoon. The nervy bastard even left a message.''

"Oh?''

"Some shit about how I'm supposed to know what brings him into town.''

"I'm listening.''

"Don't strain yourself,'' Armato said. "That's it. Some kind of two-bit brain game.''

"Is it?''

Nicky's eyes had narrowed down to gleaming slits. "You want to try plain English here?''

"We know this boy's excitable. Somebody brushes up against him in a crowded elevator, and he takes their head off. Who knows what sets him off? Some kind of hassle. Maybe he gets pissed off when someone takes his name in vain.''

"I'll say this once—I haven't made a move on Patsy yet. And if I did, I wouldn't have to hide behind a fucking marksman's medal.''

"That was the consensus in New York, but what the hell—I had to ask.''

"It crossed my mind that Patsy might've set this up himself. Dust off a couple of his troops and rig the rest of it, assuming everybody else would point the finger back at me. We both know it's been done before.''

"And Bolan?''

"Christ, you're asking me? For all I know, the fucker swallowed Patsy's line. You wanna know what Bolan's thinking, I can't help you.''

"Someone torched a couple of Scimone's cars this afternoon. I guess you heard?''

"That wasn't me. I won't pretend I'm sorry, but I haven't raised a hand against Chicago yet. I swear to God.''

"That's interesting. It makes you wonder who's been setting off the fireworks.''

"Put my money on Chicago.''

"It's a thought. I don't mind saying that New York would feel more comfortable if they knew why Bolan was in town.''

"Ask Patsy.''

"I might do that. In the meantime, you are holding up all right?''

"We're pretty solid. I was thinking maybe I should call L.A. and have them send some troubleshooters out.''

"It couldn't hurt.''

"You think so?''

"No one's gonna fault you for protecting what you own.''

"That's good to know.''

"I'll have to make some calls, but chances are that I could have a tour group out here in a day or two.''

Armato frowned, uncomfortable with the thought of friendly soldiers—friends or otherwise—descending on his territory.

"I don't know. I'd have to ask L.A."

"Okay, whatever." Bolan rose to leave. "I'll be in touch tomorrow."

Nicky trailed him to the study door and shook his hand again. "I'm glad we had this chance to sort things out," he said.

"It isn't over yet. Pagano gets a notion in his head, it's bound to stay there for a while."

"There's different ways of shaking notions. People change their minds. Sometimes they just get old and die."

"It happens. I just hope this Bolan thing won't blow up in your face."

"We're looking into it," Armato said. "I don't anticipate a problem."

"I'm relieved to see you taking care of business."

"It's the only way to go."

"Tomorrow, then."

"Tomorrow."

Bolan's escort showed him to the door and watched him slide behind the Volvo's wheel. The gate man he had spoken to a short time earlier saluted as he passed, and Bolan filed the gesture in his mind for future reference.

Retreating from the Lakewood suburb, Bolan thought Armato had appeared sincere in his confusion when it came to marksman's medals and the raids against Scimone. If he had Valentina stashed away somewhere, his motives were obscure, and he had proved himself a better actor than the Executioner had bargained for.

So much for speculation.

Nicky might have been behind the snatch in Sheridan despite his show of wide-eyed innocence, but for the moment Bolan was inclined to seek his answers elsewhere.

Perhaps, he thought, the pointman for Chicago might oblige.

6

"I hear you.... Right, of course... I understand *padrone*. Just as you say.... I will.... Goodbye."

Pasquale Scimone replaced the telephone receiver in its cradle, scowling at the instrument as if it were a mortal enemy. His ear was burning from the angry chewing-out that Don Pagano had delivered, via Ma Bell, from Chicago, and he needed someone he could take it out on, fast. Shit always rolls downhill.

He punched the intercom and snapped, "Get in here, will you?"

Rocco Fanelli, his good right hand, was first to cross the office threshold. Bringing up the rear were three crew chiefs, looking like they'd all just had their asses whipped and were waiting for an instant replay. As they settled into chairs, Scimone allowed his own to rotate, facing toward the giant picture window that provided him a view of downtown Denver. Lights were coming on out there, with the purple dusk encroaching.

Under any other circumstances, it would be his favorite time of day.

"I've just been on the phone with Don Pagano," he informed them, swiveling around to face his audience. "You want to guess what kind of mood he's in?"

No answer came from the grim quartet.

"That's right," Scimone said. "He's mad as hell, and you can take my word on that. He asked me if I thought that I was up to dealing with our little problem here. In other words, he wants to know if I'm on top of things, or if I've got my head stuck up my ass."

More silence from the troops.

"Now, I've already told the capo I can handle it—which means I told him *we* can handle it. You get my drift?"

Four solemn faces nodded.

Scimone tried a plastic smile for size. "So, what I want from all of you is very simple." He paused for effect. "I want someone to tell me *what the fuck is going on*!"

Fanelli raised his hand just like a kid in school, then caught himself and jerked it back.

"What is it, Rocco?"

"Well, we know whoever hit the storefront used some kind of military shit. It wasn't dynamite or plastics on a timer. More like rockets or grenades, some kind of deal like that. His rifle was an automatic two-two-three, so figure on an M-16, an Armalite, maybe a Ruger Mini-14. Whatever, he knows how to handle his hardware."

"But no one was hit, am I right?"

"I don't think he was trying to hit them," Fanelli replied, and the others were nodding like spring-loaded toys on a dashboard. "He wanted a chance to clear out, so he just pinned them down for a while."

"And that bit with the cars, what was that?"

"Well, it could be a warning, you know? Like a 'Get out, or else' kind of thing. Someone letting us know they can go all the way if they have to."

"That fucking Armato."

Fanelli was hesitant, shrugging. The crew chiefs just looked back and forth from Scimone to his tough number two, saying zip.

"You don't think so?"

"I have to be honest, boss. I don't know *who* we've been stepping on here. There's this thing with the medal—"

"Two bucks in a surplus store, Rocco, you said that yourself. It means nothing."

"I know, but it's still hard to figure. We've been here three months, and Armato's been walking on eggs. Then, within a few days we've got two soldiers dead—with the medal—and now all these cars blown to shit with grenades or what have you. It's happened so fast that I feel like we're dealing with somebody new.''

"What would Bolan be doing in Denver?"

"What does he do anywhere?"

Scimone didn't have to answer that. The guy kicked ass, that's what, no matter *where* he was.

"I understand that Nicky had some trouble at his club on Colorado."

"We don't have any details yet," Fanelli said. "A couple of his boys got whacked, but no one's saying who or why."

Scimone was glaring at his crew chiefs. "This had better not be someone's bright idea of getting even for the boys we lost."

"No, sir."

"No way, boss."

"Uh-uh."

"If I find out someone's letting contracts on his own, without my say-so, he can kiss his ass goodbye. We understand each other?"

"Right."

"Sure thing, boss."

"Yo."

"All right, then. If we *have* got Bolan here in town, we need to find out what the bastard wants and think about a way of stopping him. I guess you don't need me to tell you what his head's worth. Even with inflation out the ass, you bag this boy, you're ready to retire. Now, I've been wondering—"

Scimone was on the verge of polling his subordinates to sample their opinions on the likelihood of Nick Armato forming an alliance with the Executioner, but he was interrupted by a brittle cracking sound. Before he had a chance to register the broken picture window, Benny Rizzo—on his right—slumped sideways in his chair, the left side of his skull exploding into crimson slush.

Scimone was gaping at the mess when mangler number two caught Frank Pedilla in the chest and punched a fist-sized exit wound beneath his arm while the body flopped like a game fish, slinging blood all over everything.

"Get down, for Christ's sake!"

Patsy hit the floor and managed to wriggle underneath his desk about the time the picture window came apart, thick blades of glass descending like a hundred guillotines. The distant sound of rifle fire was unmistakable, some kind of heavy big-game piece. The hot incoming rounds that tunneled through his desk and the surrounding walls struck home like hammer blows delivered by a giant.

Huddled on the floor, Scimone heard Rocco crawling past him, fumbling blindly for the intercom and shouting down the line for reinforcements. "Get some people on the fucking roof!" he bawled. "And check those fucking roofs across the street! You oughta see his muzzle-flash from there."

As if on cue, the rolling thunder died away and the sound of drumming impact ceased. Beneath his desk Scimone gave the sniper sixty seconds to reload, then took another thirty to decide that it was over.

He emerged from cover cautiously and nearly stepped on what was left of Rudy Greco. Never knew what hit him, from the dazed expression on the right side of his face. The left side had been sheared away above the nostril, leaving Rudy out of kilter like a puzzle someone had forgotten to complete.

Scimone was trembling, and he sat down in his bullet-punctured swivel chair to hide the nervous spasms from Fanelli. Rocco didn't need to know the boss had nearly soiled his pants while he was under fire.

"I want this bastard," he announced, relieved to hear his voice as strong as ever. "I don't give a shit if it was Bolan, Nicky's people or the fucking Mormon Tabernacle Choir. Chicago doesn't take this crap from anybody."

Scowling at the carnage spread around him, Patsy knew that it was good to be alive.

He also knew that it was payback time.

Mack Bolan caught the news on Alameda Avenue, returning from his face-to-face with Nick Armato. He had tuned the Volvo's FM radio to easy listening for background noise to help him think, and Animotion's sounds were interrupted by the special bulletin.

"Three dead this evening, in a downtown sniping incident at Sixteenth and Arapahoe. Police have not identified the victims, pending notice to the next of kin, and homicide detectives have no comment on reports that the intended target of the shooting may have been reputed gangland figure Pasquale 'Patsy' Scimone, of Chicago."

"From the evidence available so far, it would appear that one or more assassins opened fire within the past half-hour from the roof of the Prudential Plaza, shooting toward an office building on the north side of Arapahoe. Again, we have no confirmation of the rumors pointing toward a gangland execution, but authorities confirm that three men have been killed by rifle fire. I'm Sally Fletcher, and we'll have more details for you when we break for news again at eight o'clock."

The music came back on with early Beatles, and he shut it off. His mind was racing, trying different puzzle pieces on for size, rejecting each in turn as it refused to fit.

Armato had been ready for a move against Scimone, but it was happening too fast. Eleven minutes since their little chat, and Bolan didn't think that Nicky could have put a man—or men—in place so rapidly. And then, aside from practical considerations, sniping did not strike him as Armato's style.

It sounded more like something Bolan himself would have done.

He wondered whether the police would find a marksman's medal at the scene, or if the shooter would rely on their imagination to complete the link.

It wouldn't take a genius to connect the various attacks, and Bolan wondered how much longer it would be before he saw his name in headlines. More importantly he wondered how Chicago's man in Denver would respond to the attack.

When it had been two soldiers dead, with a convenient finger pointing at the Executioner, he had been willing to regard Scimone as one more suspect in the case. A sniping raid against the mobster's office—and presumably against the man himself—was something else. While Bolan could not rule out a diversionary tactic absolutely, he was less inclined to buy the double-play scenario with five of Scimone's men dead and Patsy on the firing line.

That brought him back to Nick Armato, but the self-styled boss of Denver had appeared sincere when he denied involvement in the early "Bolan raid" against Scimone. Granted, Armato might be lying, but his shock and anger had the ring of truth about them. If the guy was acting, it was Oscar time.

Which brought the warrior back to Val and his initial problem, lacking any clues on which way he should turn. The execution of Scimone's gunners clearly meshed with her abduction, and the plan included drawing Bolan into Denver—but for what? And who was handling the play backstage?

A wild card.

Bolan's fingers tightened on the steering wheel as he confronted the worst-case scenario. If he was right, if there was yet another player in the game—still unidentified—the difficulty of his task would automatically be multiplied a hundred times.

A wild card meant that he would have to start from scratch on motive, tossing all his early preconceptions out the window. Never mind about Armato's hatred for Scimone or the Chicago family's hunger for a brand-new territory. With a stranger in the game, the motive might be anything from power politics to personal revenge, and Bolan wouldn't know for sure until he managed to identify his enemy.

The worst part was that he had nothing solid in the way of leads. In Sheridan a nameless scar-faced gunner—or a gunner in a mask—had tagged Jack Gray, abducted Val and left a signpost pointing to the Denver battlefield. In Colorado someone had been mimicking the Bolan style, apparently in hopes of touching off a full-scale war between Armato and Scimone. That much was clear.

And it made no damn sense at all.

As Bolan drove, he scanned a mental list of capos who might benefit from open war between Chicago and Los Angeles. New York was fond of double-dealing, but the Families there were eyeball-deep in federal prosecutions, already working overtime to keep from losing what they had. San Francisco was a long shot, understaffed and disinclined toward territorial expansion during recent years. The Kansas City Mob was closer, more aggressive, but informants in the ranks had failed to turn up any indication of a westward push. The southern branches of the family tree, in Houston and New Orleans, each had problems of their own with competition from Colombia, Peru and Ecuador.

And that left . . . what?

Someone had taken time to track Val down—no simple task, itself—because of her connection with the Executioner. A phony Bolan strike in Denver could have been accomplished with the marksman's medal by itself. A personal appearance was superfluous, if all the wild card wanted was a shooting war between Armato and Scimone. Abducting Val and bringing her to Denver—if she *was* in Denver—made it personal.

The conversation with Brognola echoed through his mind.

"We're pretty sure he had some facial scars."

"What kind of scars?"

"Like skin grafts. Tight and shiny, anyway."

The grim description didn't fit with any of the living enemies he knew about, offhand. A relative of someone he had taken out, perhaps, or a survivor of the Bolan wars who carried marks and memories like lethal baggage, waiting for a chance to even up the score.

At that rate, Bolan thought, it could be anyone.

He wiped the mental slate and started over, working on a plan of action. In the absence of a clear-cut target, Bolan was presented with a narrow range of options. He could loiter on the sidelines, waiting for the action to heat up between Armato and Scimone, or he could lend a hand and see what floated to the top when things began to boil.

It took him all of half a second to decide.

Inaction gave his enemies the edge, and Bolan hadn't come this far to stand by idly watching while the game played out before him. It was time to raise the ante, to discover who would stay and who would fold.

Val's life was in the pot, and he would have to play the cards as they were dealt if he had any hope of winning her away from her abductor.

In the process he might teach his enemies a thing or two.

The Executioner still had some aces up his sleeve.

7

She woke in darkness, and her first coherent thoughts became a catalog of pain. There were gradations, variations on a theme, and she took several moments to define them all. If nothing else, the process reaffirmed that she was still alive.

For openers her head was throbbing with a dull, insistent ache behind the eyes. An aftertaste of chemicals reminded her of needles and the bruising at her elbow, where the hypodermic's first two thrusts had missed the vein. She felt a surge of nausea and fought it down, continuing her inventory of discomforts.

She was stiff and sore from lying in the same position over several hours on the unyielding floor beneath her. There was nagging pressure on her bladder, and she clamped her knees together in an automatic reflex action. She was not about to let the bastard see her soil herself.

At least her hands no longer ached, and Val was startled to discover that the cuffs had been removed while she was out. She flexed her fingers gratefully, sensation coming back. If she could only find a weapon now....

The thought, coming out of nowhere, surprised her, and she pulled up short. Before she thought of fighting—even of escape—she had to find out where she was.

Probably a house.

She sensed that much, deciding that a motel would have been too risky for her captor, while a condo or apartment would have registered the sounds of neighbors getting on about their lives. A car rolled past outside from time to time, but spotty traffic verified her first impression of a residential neighborhood.

Val had no way of calculating time, and so could not deduce how far she had been abducted from her home. For all she knew, they might still be in Sheridan, and yet . . .

The memories came flooding back in bits and pieces, trailers from a violent film she wouldn't walk across the street to watch if she was given any kind of choice. She saw the man in black, his pistol holding her attention as her eyes adjusted to the sudden light, his face still out of focus. Handcuffs biting at her wrists. A stumbling passage through the hallway, past the bathroom, where she caught a glimpse of Jack—

Oh, God!

There had been blood, he hadn't been moving and she only had the gunman's word that Jack was still alive. What was it he had said? Before the needle, as she huddled on the floorboard of his car and shivered from the cold, he leaned in close beside her, almost whispering.

"He's breathing, if it matters. You and me, we've got a date to keep. Your boyfriend's waiting."

None of it made any sense. She had attempted to explain that he was making a mistake—she was a married woman, had no boyfriend, and he must want someone else—but then the needle found its mark and velvet darkness swallowed her alive.

Val realized that she wasn't confined in total darkness, after all. Across the room, some fifteen feet away, a door stood partly open, with a night-light burning on the other side. A glimpse of sink and tile renewed the nagging pressure on her bladder, and she knew that it was time to move.

Conceiving motion was the easy part; achieving it was something else. Her arms and legs would not obey commands at first, and by the time she mastered them enough to rise on hands and knees, her headache had mustered the strength for a dizzying counterattack. Val braced herself on all fours, like a wounded animal, dark hair hanging in a screen around her face. If she could only keep herself from passing out...

The moment faded, and the pain became more bearable by slow degrees. Her stomach clenched, but there was nothing to disgorge. An empty threat. She traveled more than halfway to the door on hands and knees, attempting to stand upright only when she knew that she was close enough to catch herself against the jab if she began to fall.

One leg, and then the other. Simple, once she hitched the hemline of her tangling nightgown up around her knees. But now the room was spinning, and she had to brace herself against the wall until the rush of dizziness subsided. As she edged across the threshold, the linoleum was cool beneath bare feet.

She found the light switch, flicked it on, recoiling from her own reflection in the mirror. First the toilet, while she still had time. Before the man in black returned, perhaps with needles.

A man in black.

"Your boyfriend's waiting."

There was something nagging at her, lurking in a shadowed corner of her mind, but Val lost track of it as she relieved herself. There was a combination tub-and-shower to her right, complete with towels and soap—the motel size, still wrapped—and she was captivated by the notion of a steaming bath to soak her aches and pains away.

But she couldn't take the chance. Her captor might barge in at any moment, and she wouldn't let him catch her in the nude. Her flannel nightgown wasn't much, but it afforded more protection than her birthday suit.

She caught herself before she flushed the toilet—*don't make any noise, not yet*—and steeled herself to give the mirror one more try, as though her appearance would give her a clue to understand just what was happening.

All things considered, she was holding up okay. Her hair was mussed and tangled, but a brush would put that right if she could ever get her hands on one. The smudges on her face were dirt, perhaps from lying on the floorboard of her jailer's car. The right sleeve of her nightgown had been ripped above the elbow, and she noted several blood spots on the flannel, but the puncture wounds had scabbed without a trace of complications.

Overall, despite some latent dizziness and nausea, Val felt reasonably fit. She had been fortunate in one respect. In her unconscious state, the stranger could have—

She quickly blocked the train of thought as she began to conjure images of pale hands slipping underneath her nightgown.

Val tried the medicine cabinet and found it empty. Ditto the drawers and cabinet under the sink, which yielded a single dead roach for her effort. No brush or comb. No weapons, natch.

If only she had something she could use in self-defense. And what would Mack have done?

Suddenly she understood as the scarred man's words echoed in her mind again. *"Your boyfriend's waiting."* There had been no mistake. She had been chosen, coldly and deliberately, as bait. It was the only answer that made any sense at all.

But *how*? Security was Jack's department, and they had been safe for years. So long, in fact, that there were days, and sometimes weeks, when Val thought nothing of the danger that had marred her past. It was a given constant, like the bomb or air pollution, and you couldn't spend each moment of your life in trembling fear.

It was amazing how times changed.

She had been living in a dreamworld, heedless of the savages around her on the night Mack Bolan came into her life. How long ago? Val didn't like to think about it. Standing on her porch in robe and slippers, calling for her cat, when he appeared from nowhere, all in black and packing weapons, drenched in blood along one side.

Somehow she had believed him when he told her that it would be death for him—for both of them—if she alerted the police. The telephone was there when he lost consciousness, exhausted from his struggle and the loss of blood, but she had tended to his wound instead of calling the authorities. And slowly, surely, she began to nurse him back to health.

He told her who he was before the headlines had a chance, and Val surprised herself again by understanding his crusade. She had opposed the war in Vietnam on principle, and violent movies turned her off, but she was somehow able to accept the logic of a warrior who had executed dozens—hundreds—of his fellow men. Alone in the world since the age of twenty, she had recognized his pain at losing three-fourths of his family, the urge to seek revenge, but at a deeper level, Val had seen that Bolan wasn't any trigger-happy vigilante on a rampage.

He was fighting for a cause, and it became *her* cause when sympathy and caring blossomed into love.

Mack had a brother, age fourteen, in need of shelter from the coming storm. She had responded automatically, without a moment's conscious thought for inconvenience or the danger to herself. When Bolan gave her cash and documents, a brand new life, she had accepted them, no questions asked. She waved his thanks away and wept when Bolan ordered her to think of him as one already dead.

In Boston, when a careless oversight had nearly got Val and Johnny killed, it had been Mack who sought them out and purged their enemies with fire. She had not seen him since, but there was always Johnny, growing fast and strong, with so much of his brother in him that it sometimes made her cry.

Jack Gray had taken Valentina by surprise. A federal officer assigned to her protection detail after Mack and Hal Brognola cut an off-the-record deal, Jack held himself aloof at first, solicitous but cool. Protecting Val had been a job, like covering a witness, checking fingerprints or running down a stolen car. It took some time for him to loosen up, and by the time he really noticed her, he had been hooked.

Val needed time herself, although for different reasons. Slowly but surely, she felt herself attracted to the G-man with the sandy hair and quirky smile, but every time she let herself relax, the guilt came back to haunt her. Mack was out there somewhere, dying day by day, while she aspired to something like a normal life. It wasn't fair, and Johnny's presence only made her feelings seem more treacherous.

In time, when she could not deny the warmth—and yes, the love—she felt for Jack, she laid the problem out for Johnny, trusting him to understand. He hadn't disappointed her, although she held her breath when he had traveled to St. Louis with Brognola for a hurried meeting with his brother. Johnny brought Mack's words to Val, verbatim: "Wish me well, John. And tell me goodbye. Then go wish Val well. And tell her thanks."

The misplaced guilt had lingered for a time, and Johnny felt some measure of the same, but they had helped each other through it, talking out the rough spots, holding on to one another through it all. As time went by, recriminations faded, disappeared, and each of them had come to private terms with loss. With the realities of building up a new life, day by day.

The years with Jack had been a peaceful, loving time, but she had followed Bolan's war in headlines when he surfaced. She'd been briefed by Hal in preparation for the sham of Bolan's "death" in New York City and his later reappearance on the public scene. There had been Johnny in the meantime, and she swallowed her objections when he joined the Seabees, serving time in Lebanon. She knew that John was mixed up in his brother's war somehow these days, but Val had never asked the details. Jack had loved her well through all of it, and she had loved him in return.

But at the same time, she had never quite stopped loving Mack.

You never quite forget your first, or so they said, and while he had not been the first to occupy her bed, Mack Bolan *was* the first man who had ever truly captured Valentina's heart. The love she felt for Jack was tempered by the flames that she had passed through on her way to reach him. Suffering and loss. The bittersweet delight of making

love for what may be the last time in your life. The strain
and fear of living on the edge.

It would have taken time, expense and effort for her abductor to run her down. The paper trail existed, certainly,
but it was camouflaged with phony twists and turns along
the way to throw pursuers off the track. It was a testimony
to the enemy's resourcefulness that he had come this far.

She wished him dead and roasting in the fires of hell.

The fires.

His face and hands . . .

Burn scars.

The fleeting memory produced a shudder of revulsion.
Valentina wondered if his injuries were linked somehow to
his profession as a gunman, but she finally decided that it
didn't matter. He had wounded Jack, and her mind recoiled in horror from the possibility that Jack was dead. He
had abducted her, and it was plain from where she stood
that he was bent on killing Bolan.

Mack or John?

Dear God, could he be after *both*?

She put a rein on her imagination, checking it before she
fell apart. Survival was the first priority, and living through
a crisis situation meant you kept your wits about you. Leave
the fantasies alone and focus every waking thought on getting out of here alive.

In the larger room she found another light switch and
spent a moment examining her cell. No windows. Nothing
in the way of furniture or carpeting. An outside lock secured the only other door. The closet had been stripped of
hangers, hooks and rod.

So much for self-defense.

She had her hands and feet, if it came down to that,
against at least one man supplied with guns and stupefying
drugs. She could resist him if he came with more injec-
tions, but he might decide to kill her for convenience if she
gave him any trouble.

But he wanted her alive, or she would certainly be dead by
now. He could have killed her at the house, or any time since

he had carried her away. There had been ample time for him to chop her up and hide the pieces if her own short-term survival didn't figure in his plans.

But he would kill her when his job was done. Of that, Val had not the slightest doubt. By definition, live bait was expendable.

And what would Mack do in her place?

Assess his situation for escape potential and the possibility of laying hands on makeshift weapons.

Check.

Discern the motives of his enemy and use that knowledge to discover any weakness that he might exploit to personal advantage.

Check.

She had been snatched to lure Bolan out of hiding, as a prelude to assassination. In a pinch she might be able to derail the plan with physical resistance or—

The idea of suicide was alien to Val, but she reviewed it as a last-ditch option. If her enemies could only make the ambush work with living bait, and she could find no way of breaking free...well, it was worthy of consideration. She could always smash the bathroom mirror, use the wicked sliver of her choice to open vital arteries and veins.

It was a sad, repugnant thought, but it came down to trade-offs in the end. If she was bound to die in any case, and living for a few more hours meant the death of one she loved, then Val believed that she could check out with a smile. It was enough to know that Mack would punish them for everything.

Having considered the option, she shelved it for the time being. Val wasn't finished yet, not by any means. And when it came to mirror-smashing time, she might decide to use those wicked slivers on her enemies instead. No point in checking out before you took a stab at evening the score.

Val had no formal training in the martial arts, but along the way she had learned some moves from Jack. Aside from living under cover, it was still a rough, tough world out there, and she could take care of herself.

She tried the door once more and cursed beneath her breath.

Okay. If she was trapped, at least the flip side meant she had the two rooms to herself for now. Her enemies would have to come and get her when the time rolled around, and they might not find her ready to oblige.

Val killed the lights and settled down to wait.

8

It would be tempting fate to call on Scimone, but Bolan had no choice. Before he could eliminate Chicago's strongman as a suspect in the Sheridan abduction, he would have to see Scimone face-to-face to get a reading on his personal involvement in the game.

Some game.

Not counting the three Armato goons Bolan had taken out himself, there were five dead already. And while mobsters in the morgue upset Mack Bolan not at all, he *was* concerned about a stranger making hits on his behalf. It had been tried in other Mafia campaigns, almost from the beginning of his private war, as different capos tried to lay the blame for unrelated crimes at Bolan's door. Sometimes they killed each other, hiding lethal power politics behind the shadow of the Executioner. In several instances the targets had been public figures, randomly selected to embarrass Bolan and produce official heat.

He still had no coherent reading on the Denver game, but intuition told him that Armato and Scimone were not the only players. It was still a hunch, without foundation in objective fact, but Bolan meant to test it by the only means available.

According to Brognola, Patsy had a place on Windsor Lake, about ten miles from Nick Armato's Lakewood stronghold. Bolan drove around the residential neighborhood awhile to get its feel and verify escape routes, first checking out the capo's bastion from a safe distance before he made his move.

The fence was black wrought-iron, approximately eight feet tall, with spikes on top. It offered little in the way of privacy, as far as gawkers were concerned, but it would be a bitch to climb. Inside, strategic shade trees screened a mansion roughly twice the size of Nick Armato's. It was an older structure, much like the setting for a grade-B film about a haunted house.

Four soldiers on the gate, and given Patsy's recent problems, Bolan figured there would be at least an equal number in the nearby trees, prepared to serve as backup. All of them were giving him the bad eye as he braked outside the gate, with hands inside their jackets as though they all had chronic indigestion. Heartburn with a Magnum load.

He waited while they muttered back and forth among themselves, deciding who should take a chance and step outside the fence. The winner wasn't overjoyed by his selection, but he was outnumbered and apparently outranked. Two gunners covered him while a third drew back the left side of the double gate just far enough to let him out.

The guy was on display now, and he made a show of swaggering as he approached the car. A glance in the direction of his cronies reassured the scout that they were keeping an eye on him.

"What's up?" he asked. Too cool.

"Your number, if I don't get in to see the man damn quick. We're wasting time."

His answer took the gate man by surprise, and Bolan watched the guy's expression run the gamut from surprise and anger to a wary kind of curiosity, the shift complete in something like a second and a half.

"Nobody sees the man without a clearance," Mr. Cool replied. He didn't know what he was dealing with, but he recalled procedure well enough to stand his ground.

"I think this ought to do the trick," said Bolan, handing him the death card. "Name's Omega. Would you shake a leg and pass that on to someone with authority?"

The guy had angry color in his cheeks, but he wasn't prepared to argue with an Ace. "Hang on a second, will ya?"

"I've got nowhere else to go."

It boiled down to a fair approximation of the scene that he had played outside Armato's place, with twice the audience. They passed the card around, all nonchalance, but they kept glancing back at Bolan as if he had two heads. One of them faded back to use a telephone or radio, and when he reappeared, his attitude had changed. The boys were stepping lively, drawing back the gates, when Mr. Cool returned with Bolan's calling card.

"They're waiting for you at the house, sir. Straight along the drive, there. You can't miss it."

Bolan didn't bother thanking him before he pulled away. It was a hundred yards between the gate and house, but following the drive he traveled twice that far along a looping path between the trees. His headlights picked out sentries here and there, some packing shotguns, others armed with automatic rifles.

Patsy wasn't taking any chances. It was good to know.

It also tended to reinforce his first impression that Scimone was not responsible for the attacks upon his own brigade.

A final curve, more trees, and then the manor house loomed up before him. Old but well maintained, it stood three stories tall, with rambling wings to either side. There were more unattached buildings in the back—perhaps a barn or large garage, with smaller sheds besides—and Bolan figured that Scimone could house an army on the grounds if he was so inclined. Thus far he saw no evidence of major troop deployment, but Chicago wasn't all that far away by air.

Three guns were waiting for him out in front. One held the door for Bolan and offered to park the Volvo, but the warrior shook his head and kept the keys. It wouldn't make much difference if the play went sour, but he didn't like surrendering the smallest edge.

"Good evening, sir." The man in charge sounded smoothly practiced. "If you would follow me...."

Inside, the house smelled like old money once removed. It could have used an airing, but the musty atmosphere seemed *right*, somehow, as if it matched the woodwork and the carpeting, the paintings on the walls. His escort started up a curving staircase with Bolan on his heels and two guns bringing up the rear.

Upstairs the artwork ran to seascapes, and the walls were papered in a rich brocade. Their destination was a large room on the second floor, where the walls were lined with mounted game and fishing trophies on wooden plaques. He wondered if Scimone was a sportsman as he noticed the layer of dust accumulated on the trophies, then decided that they must have been a package deal, included with the lease.

"Mr. Scimone will join you shortly, sir."

The house man didn't ask if he was packing, but he left the scowling bookends at the open doorway, scoping Bolan's every move. He managed to ignore them, picked out a recliner done in cowhide and relaxed with his feet up. Waiting for the man.

Scimone blew in a moment later, five foot nine and stocky, moving with the restless energy of someone who had sampled life inside a cage. That would have been the two-year stretch in Joliet, thought Bolan, or perhaps the thirty-seven months in Leavenworth.

"Omega, is it?"

Bolan didn't rise to greet his host. "That's right. You want the card?"

"Seen one, you've seen 'em all," Scimone replied. He turned to face the bookends. "You can close the door and wait outside," he said. "I don't think anybody's getting wasted here tonight."

Chicago's front man settled in a chair across from Bolan, separated from his uninvited guest by ten or fifteen feet. "I'm betting this is not a social call," he said.

"You'd win that bet."

"So, give. What brings an Ace to Denver on a night like this?"

"You got complaints about the weather, Patsy?"

If Scimone was stung by the familiarity, he let it pass. The guy had other problems on his mind. "Damn right I've got complaints. The last few days, it's raining bombs and bullets here. I've lost five boys and half a dozen cars, I've got commercial property all shot to shit—you bet your ass I've got complaints."

"That's why I'm here."

"You're Mr. Fix-it, huh?"

"Let's say I make a point of tracking problems to their source."

"You could've saved yourself a trip. I *know* the source."

"That so?"

"It don't take Sherlock Holmes to figure out who's on my case. Some people can't abide a little healthy competition."

"Meaning Nick Armato?"

"I don't mean *Saint* Nick."

"Word has it that you've got another problem on your hands."

"Oh, yeah?"

"A little Bolan action, for example."

"Pull the other one," Scimone sneered. "You want to know what I think? Nicky wants a shooting war, but he's afraid to face Chicago on his own. He sends a gofer to the Army-surplus store and gets himself some trinkets he can throw away to make it look like Bolan's buying in. He pops a couple of my buttons on the corner, drops a marksman's medal—bingo. Bolan's back in town."

"So, what about your storefront?"

"What about it? You want M-16s? You want grenades? No problem. I got plenty of my own. This Bolan's not the only guy around who's holding hardware, if you get my drift."

"And you think Nicky crashed your party at the office there?"

"I think he *had* it done, hell, yes. Who's asking all these questions, anyway? Besides yourself, I mean."

"You know the way things work. I get a call, they say go here, go there. I follow orders, Patsy, just like you."

"You're saying the Commission's in on this?"

"They're interested. Nobody needs a war right now. Especially they don't need Bolan ripping up the country-side."

"Forget about him. It's a pipe dream, let me tell you. Nicky thinks he's pulling off a fast one with this Bolan crap."

"It doesn't read that way from where I'm standing."

"Oh?"

"Fact is, we have good reason to believe you may have company in Denver."

"Yeah? Says who?"

"We've got our sources, Patsy. Just say we've triple-checked, and it keeps coming out the same way every time."

"Well, shit." Scimone was frowning now, rethinking strategies. "Why me, for Christ's sake?"

"Funny you should ask that question. I was working up to that myself."

"It makes no sense to me," Scimone protested. "Jeez, we're penny-rate here. The bastard wants to take Chicago on, why don't he *hit* Chicago?"

"Maybe he gets pissed about Chicago branching out. Some other people I could mention feel the same."

"The last I heard, this town was open territory."

"Open's one thing," Bolan told him. "Taking over is another. Some folks say Chicago doesn't like to share. They say a certain capo wants the whole thing for himself."

"Is that what *you* say?"

Bolan shrugged. "I haven't made my mind up yet. Right now I'm concentrating on this other problem."

"So? You gonna keep me in suspense or what?"

"Thing is, some people worry that you may have brought this Bolan trouble on yourself, and they're afraid the guy may still be pissed when he gets done with you."

"You're doing wonders for my confidence."

"I'm just an echo, Patsy."

"Right. So, what's the game? How is it I supposedly pissed Bolan off?"

"I don't have all the details, right offhand. Word is that Bolan has himself a friend. A *girl*friend."

"Hey, a little something on the side. All right."

"Whatever. Anyhow, the last few years, she's tried to make herself invisible."

"I can't imagine why."

"The punch line is that someone found her, and they've got her in the bag. This someone even took the time to leave a note, says he was taking her to Denver. Anything about this ring a bell?"

"Why should it?"

"Way we figure, Bolan's hot to find his little friend and step on anybody in the way. It looks more like a setup all the time."

"You want to spell that out?"

"It's simple two-plus-two. Somebody snatches Bolan's squeeze, next thing you know he's kicking ass—*your* ass—like there was no tomorrow. How's that look to you?"

"You're saying *I* brought Mack the Bastard into Denver?"

"Well—"

"That's crazy. Why the hell would I do that?"

"One theory is, you meant to lay it off on Nicky, but your boys fucked up."

"Bull*shit*! We're pointing fingers here, so why couldn't Nicky bag the broad and try to lay it off on me? That makes more sense, I'd say, considering my boys have taken all the lumps so far."

"You ask me, Patsy, it could still go either way."

"I don't believe this."

"There's another possibility, of course."

"What's that?"

"A wild card." Bolan saw confusion on the mobster's face and forged ahead. "Somebody wants to hurt the brotherhood, for instance, and they've got it in for Bolan, too. What better way to score than playing off both ends against the middle?''

"You've been reading too much science fiction, guy."

"Just think about it. The alternative says you or Nicky."

"Put my money on Armato."

"Either way, your buddies on the board get mad enough, they might start flipping coins."

"A wild card, huh?"

"It's just a possibility. I thought I'd ask."

"Nobody comes to mind, but I could check around."

"That might not be a bad idea."

"Okay, but in the meantime—"

"I know what you're saying," Bolan interrupted. "It's an open territory, like you say, and everybody's got a right to self-defense."

"That's how I see it."

"Fair is fair. The only thing I'd hate to see is lots of heat from people getting wasted right and left, you follow? At the moment, *La Commissione* is undecided which way they should jump. Some of them side with California—hey, you've got to figure that, okay? A couple of the others like Chicago, but the bulk of them are playing wait-and-see. They want this Bolan shit resolved, and after that . . .''

"Go on."

"I think once that's resolved, the board will line up on the winning side."

"That's good to know."

"Of course, I wouldn't be surprised if a couple of them want to wet their beaks. You understand the way things work."

"Hell, yes. That's understood. You want to keep things rolling, grease the wheels."

"Exactly."

"I appreciate your coming out to see me here."

"My pleasure," Bolan said.

"Okay. This other thing, I'll make inquiries. If there's someone with a hard-on for the brotherhood, he's gotta have a name."

"One thing I didn't mention."

"Yeah?"

"There was a witness on the snatch. Guy stopped a couple, but he's still alive. We don't know whether that was accidental or intentional."

"I'm listening."

"He says the shooter had some kind of scars around his face, like maybe skin grafts. I don't know. That may not be for sure. It's something, anyway."

"I guess."

Scimone was frowning to himself, whether in concentration or out of recognition, Bolan couldn't say.

"Whatever. Food for thought. You never know what might be helpful on a deal like this."

"I hear you."

On his feet he shook hands with Scimone and let the mobster trail him to the doorway, where the bookends waited just outside.

"I'll be in touch."

"You want my number here?"

"I've got your number, Patsy."

"Right, okay." But he was frowning as though he didn't quite enjoy the sound of that. "It's bound to take a while, but I'll get on it right away."

"That's all I ask."

"I'll see you, then."

"I wouldn't be surprised."

The house man led him back along the corridor, their escort trailing a respectful distance to the rear. It didn't pay to mess around with someone who could bait the boss like that and walk away from it with all his body parts intact. Times change, and bosses, too. A soldier never knew which side his bread was buttered on from one day to the next.

He found the Volvo waiting where he left it, thanked the house man for his courtesy and drove away. The gates were standing open when he got there, sentries well away to either side. Not taking any chances with an Ace.

As Bolan put the place behind him, he replayed his conversation with Scimone. The guy was certainly a shark, but he appeared sincere in his attempt to blame Armato for the "Bolan" strikes. His shock at being implicated in the move on Val seemed genuine enough, and that left Bolan reshuffling the deck.

He knew Chicago wanted Denver, or a major piece of it, at any rate, and it was safe to say Los Angeles wouldn't roll over and play dead without a fight. So far, so good. He would have been content to let them kill each other off, except that Val was somewhere in the middle of it all.

It had been risky, mentioning the witness to Scimone, but Jack was under heavy guard and would remain so. Anyway, if Scimone had pulled the snatch, he knew about Val's husband going in.

That left the goddamn wild card.

Scars like skin grafts on his face.

He wished Scimone good hunting, swallowing frustration as he realized that he had managed to accomplish nothing so far.

Correction.

He had covered all the bases he could reach, establishing communications with the warring camps. Armato and Scimone each had a stake in working with the man they called Omega, and the link—if properly exploited—could make all the difference in the world.

A wild card who intended to destroy Mack Bolan *and* the Denver Mob. Or had he overlooked some larger aspect of the riddle? Did his adversary hate the syndicate at large? If so, it opened up a whole new ball game with an even larger cast of players. Viewed from that perspective, he couldn't rule out police or federal agents from the list of possibles. The wild card might be *anyone*.

He made a mental note to speak with Hal about the possibility and try to get some mileage out of the computer banks in Wonderland. Aside from that, in lieu of marking time and waiting for the other shoe to drop, he had to act.

An unknown enemy had taken special pains to place the Executioner in Denver, counting on the soldier to react. Whatever happened next, in terms of Val's survival and eventual return, might hinge on Bolan's personal response.

So be it.

Given the surroundings and the circumstances, he would play it true to form. The same way he had played it once before, in Boston, when a beloved's survival was riding on the line.

A Bolan blitz, damn right.

It was the only way to go.

9

Tommy Cheesecake thought it was ridiculous to go along with normal business in the face of all the shit that had been coming down the past few days. He wouldn't dream of telling that to Nicky—Mama Ciccio had not raised any fools— but it was his opinion that they ought to cool things for a while, lie low and wait to see what happened next.

Of course, nobody in the Family was asking Tommy Cheesecake what he thought. He was a simple button, standing somewhere near the bottom of the heap, and his opinion didn't count for shit. They called him Cheesecake for his looks—the soulful eyes and wavy hair, and a smile that charmed the pants off half the women Tommy knew— but being handsome didn't mean he was retarded. Tommy Cheesecake knew which way the wind was blowing, bet your ass, and he could read the writing on the wall.

He knew, for instance, that Chicago was intent on gobbling Denver up and booting Nicky A. out on his ass. He also knew, from listening when no one thought he knew enough to pay attention, that the Executioner was lining up some kind of action in the mile-high city. He had killed three boys and left his calling card at Nicky's upper club, on Colorado Boulevard, and if the rumors were correct, he'd done a lot worse to Chicago, bombing cars and sniping people from the rooftops.

It made no sense for Tommy Cheesecake to be on the streets at night, collecting money from assorted lowlifes, when the Family should have been preparing for a war. It wasn't bad enough they had to fight Chicago; now it looked like they would have to deal with Mack the Bastard, too. Whoever called that normal ought to have his freaking head examined.

Tommy Cheesecake hadn't been around when Bolan first declared war on the brotherhood some years previously, but he had talked to one or two survivors of the early rumble in Los Angeles. Such men were few and far between. When they agreed to speak of Bolan, they invariably came on tough as nails, describing how they'd do it differently the next time, really fry his ass, but talking "next time" made them twitchy, nervous looking, as if they'd rather climb inside a hole and pull it after them than face the guy again.

Okay, so he was tough. You had to figure that, or someone would have punched his ticket years ago. More reason why the Family should have been preparing its defenses rather than pretending there was nothing wrong. Chicago *and* Mack Bolan. Jesus.

Still, it had been Nicky's call, and Tommy Cheesecake had to figure that the boss was acting under orders from Los Angeles. That didn't help tremendously, but it was nice to know that someone else—someone with more experience, perhaps—had mulled the problem over for a while before deciding on a course of action.

Funny, though, the way it still gave Tommy Cheesecake goose bumps every time he hit the streets. As though there was someone walking on his grave.

The nightly schedule called for pickups from a dozen flunkies—pimps and dealers, for the most part—plus a drop to one of Nicky's contacts at the cop house. In return for cash, Armato picked up information and a measure of immunity, with ample warning when the city fathers had their periodic bouts of virtue and demanded "tough, decisive measures" to reduce the local crime rate. Twice a year or so, the cops would round up small-fry on the streets, and Nick would front the money for their fines. It was a part of life, like paying rent or picking up the tab for the utilities.

The drop was nothing, in and out at Denny's with the cop all stone faced, barely speaking. It was rich, the way they

came on so superior, like Mr. Clean, and all the time they
had their hands out, wanting more. For Tommy Cheesecake's money, you could have the cops. Give him an honest
wise guy any day, and shove that crap about the "thin blue
line" protecting so-called civilized society. The Mob provided goods and services demanded by the "decent" men
and women of society, and if the bluesuits ever *really* did
their job, there would be hell to pay. The so-called upper
crust, deprived of easy women, drugs and other hot com-
modities, would go to pieces overnight.

His pay off made, the rest were all collections. Two black
pimps and one Latino, operating in the city under Nicky's
wing, kicked back the standard thirty-three percent. It was
a cheap insurance policy, considering the fate of several in-
dependents who refused to play along when L.A. first began to colonize the Rocky Mountain territory. In return for
one-third of their gross, the players got a measure of police
protection, plus a guarantee that freelance whores would not
be stealing business from the streets. Above all else, they got
to stay alive, with every working part intact.

The pimps were businessmen. They understood that every
operation had its overhead, and there were seldom any beefs
about the going rate. It was a miracle, the way so many different types made out like bandits when they got behind the
spirit of free enterprise. America was really something when
you thought about it.

The rest of Tommy Cheesecake's pickups were from
dealers handling smack, cocaine, whatever. Denver was a
party town, and Nicky's team supplied the snowbirds up in
Vail and Aspen, too. Some winter weekends, Tommy would
have bet you'd find more powder smeared around on upper lips than on the slopes. It was a modern gold rush, and
the brotherhood was cashing in.

His final stop before returning to the barn was Crestmoor Park, near Lowry Air Force Base. The contact was a
sergeant or whatever they were called these days, spec
something, who was moving speed and other pharmaceuticals to customers in uniform. It was a thriving business, and

the guy was so industrious that Nicky only tapped his gross for twenty-five percent, above the cost of the supplies. Such generosity was rare, but not unheard-of in the trade.

The airman was a cocky Texas transplant, always wise-cracking and coming on with jokes that Tommy didn't follow half the time. Still, he was good at taking care of business in a pinch, and there were unconfirmed rumors that he had staged the accident that killed a CID investigator some months back. The probe of drugs on-base had been abandoned after an application of strategic grease upstairs, and that month Nicky let the guy keep eighty-five percent of what he made.

America.

The meet went down on schedule, with the sergeant grinning like he always did, amusing Tommy with a quip about Confucius, lady pilots and a hairy crack-up. Handing off the better part of eighty grand like it was chump change. Tommy Cheesecake hung around and chewed the fat awhile, obeying his instructions that included buttering the sergeant up whenever possible, and it was after ten o'clock when they split up.

A short walk from the swing set to his car, and Tommy had his keys in hand, about to stash the sergeant's payoff in the trunk—three hundred thousand dollars, give or take, in an Adidas bag—when some guy stepped up close behind him, prodding at his kidneys with the muzzle of a gun.

"Let's take a little walk," the stranger said.

There wasn't any future in resisting. Tommy Cheesecake said, "Okay, why not?"

"You'd better bring the bag."

He thought about a move while he was opening the trunk, but there was no percentage in it. Mr. X would shoot him in the back before he had a chance to pull it off, and Tommy Cheesecake didn't want to die for Nicky's money. If he saw a decent chance to save it, make a hero of himself, it wouldn't hurt to try, but suicide was stupid.

Once he had the bag in hand, the gunner let him turn around. The guy was average size and slender, but his face was creepy. Scarred around the cheeks and up one side, to where a hat was pulled down low above his eyes. Like Freddy Kruger in the *Elm Street* movies. Tommy Cheese-cake wondered if the guy went bobbing for French fries on Halloween, but he kept the thought to himself.

The scars were one thing, but the gunner's eyes were something else. The guy had psycho eyes, as if it would only take a word—perhaps a sideways glance—to make him open fire.

"The hardware," Tommy's captor said. "Left-handed. Toss it in and close the trunk."

The button did as he was told.

"Good boy. We'll take my car."

They found it half a block away, and Tommy waited while the gunner got his own trunk open, fishing handcuffs from his pocket with a right hand that reminded Tommy of a lobster's claw.

"You know the drill," the scar-faced stranger said. "Behind your back, and make 'em tight."

It was a first for Tommy Cheesecake, putting handcuffs on himself, but on the second try he got it right. Of course, he left himself a little slack, but it was wasted effort, since the gunner double-checked and cranked the ratchets tight enough to break the skin.

"Okay, get in."

"In there?"

"You heard me."

It was fucking awkward, climbing in the trunk without a hand to steady him, and Tommy Cheesecake banged his head a couple times before he got himself positioned in a fetal curl, his shoulders jammed against the spare.

"All comfy? Good."

It could be worse, thought Tommy. Anyway, I'm still alive.

And then the lid came down.

COLLECTION OF INTELLIGENCE had been Carboni's weakness from the start. Cut off from normal contacts in the brotherhood when he went underground, he had to work without the inside information that had guided him on countless contracts as an Ace. When all else failed, he had to improvise.

Selection of the Denver killing round had been a relatively simple task, with rumbles of impending trouble on the street available to anyone with ears. The rest had been surveillance, staking out Armato and Scimone to spot their homes and offices, identify their troops, but there was so much more Vince had to know before he sprang the trap on Mack the Bastard.

Bolan needed help to stir things up in Denver, and Carboni meant to lend a hand, but first he needed targets. Not the supper-club variety, but something that would hit Armato where his heart was.

In the pocketbook.

For that, Carboni needed information, and what better source than one of Nicky's trusted runners? Picking out his mark was easy, scoping gofers as they left the headshed, choosing one who looked like he was smart enough to know his business but young enough that he would be afraid to die. Vince didn't know the runner's name and didn't care. It was enough that he could walk and talk on cue.

From Crestmoor Park, Carboni drove the hostage to his safehouse, sandwiched in between the Denver Union Stockyards and Riverside Cemetery. The setting had appeal for Vince. He felt relaxed in close proximity to so much death.

Above all else, the house was isolated from its neighbors, ringed by ancient trees and gardens gone to seed. It gave him privacy, and he had stashed the woman there as soon as they returned to Denver, locked securely in an inside room, no windows, with a stout Yale padlock on the only door. Armato's runner wasn't staying long enough to rate accommodations of his own. For him the basement workshop would suffice.

It was an hour short of midnight when he killed his headlights in the covered carport. Vincent brought the heavy bag and set it on the ground beside him as he opened up the trunk. His claw could handle keys all right, with the pistol in his left hand, covering. The gofer had some trouble climbing out, but in the end he made it. Vince retrieved the bag and steered his captive toward the rear.

Inside, the gofer stood and waited while Carboni turned the lights on, pointing with his pistol toward a closet door that opened on the basement stairs. Another light switch, and the yawning pit was brightened by a pair of naked bulbs.

"I need my hands," the gofer said, examining the steep and narrow flight of stairs.

"You'll manage," Vince assured him.

He was halfway to the bottom when he slipped and lost his footing, thumping down the last eight steps and landing in an awkward sprawl below. A cut had opened on his forehead, smearing blood across his face, but he seemed otherwise unharmed.

"You'll live," Carboni told him.

The gofer struggled to his feet, and Vincent nudged him toward the center of the room, where block and tackle were suspended from a rafter. Taking care to keep the pistol pressed against his captive's skull, Carboni plied a key and pulled the cuffs away.

"Take off your clothes," he said before the gofer got a start on rubbing life into his hands.

"Say what?"

"I don't like to repeat myself."

"Okay, no problem."

He watched with disinterest as the guy shrugged off his jacket, looked around for somewhere he could hang it, finally dropping it on the concrete floor. He wore no undershirt and was so cool in his bikini briefs and nylon socks that he was shivering.

"The rest of it."

"Whatever."

Not so casual now, despite the false bravado.

Carboni dropped the handcuffs and a set of shackles on the floor beside his prisoner. "The ankles first," he ordered. "Then lie down and fix the cuffs behind your back."

The runner followed orders, and the cuffs were better this time. Vincent barely had to tighten them at all. He pulled the tackle down and hooked it underneath the chains on both the shackles and the handcuffs, stepping back a pace to scope his handiwork before he carried on.

The gofer was immobilized, facedown, his hands behind his back and legs bent at the knees. When he was hoisted five feet off the floor—no easy job, but manageable—he reminded Vince of a piñata at a carnival in Mexico. The kind you hit with sticks to find out what surprises have been tucked away inside.

No sticks for this one, though. Carboni didn't put his faith in anything so crude.

"I've got some questions for you," Vincent said. "Some information that I need, you understand? I figure you can help me out."

The gofer sounded different, hanging there, but Vince could understand him perfectly.

"I don't have anything to say about the Family."

"You're loyal. I like that in a person. Time was, the Commission took account of loyalty and rewarded guys who did their jobs. Oh, well, times change."

"I don't know who you are—the DEA, whatever—but I've got my rights."

"Damn straight. You've got the right to speak with an attorney, but I don't see one around right now. Tough break. You've got the right to keep your mouth shut, if you can. I'm betting you're too smart to sacrifice yourself for Nicky's sake."

"This won't stand up in court, man."

"Hey, I guess I'll have to take my chances."

It was dawning on the gofer now. "You ain't no cop."

"By George, I think he's got it."

"You're working for Scimone, is that the story?"

Vincent let him see the puckered scowl. "I wouldn't touch that bastard with a ten-foot pole."

"Whatever. Listen, man, you've got about three hundred thousand in the bag. That isn't bad for one night's work. You call this off, I'll tell the boss that Patsy's people made the grab. No skin off me."

"Not yet."

"It's perfect, right? Three hundred big ones and the perfect cover. Hell, I don't know who you are. I couldn't give you up, regardless."

"I've already got the money," Vince reminded him. "You're not in a position to be quoting terms."

The gofer tried to find a way around that problem, thinking fast, but there was no way out. He swallowed hard and said, "I guess you'll have to do me, then. I won't sell out the Family."

Carboni crossed the room and spent a moment at the workbench, picking out a butane torch. He lit it, took his time with the adjustment of the flame and sauntered back to stand beneath his hanging captive.

"Are you sure?"

The guy was sweating, but it wouldn't save him. Vince knew everything there was to know about the incompatibility of flame and human flesh.

"Fuck off, okay?"

"Your call."

He singed a little chest hair first, and let the gofer smell it burning. Pubic hair smelled much the same, but it was thicker. Wiry.

"Simple questions," Vincent said. "A little travelogue, or else you're going up in smoke."

"I wouldn't give you shit, you fucking *aaiiee*!"

"A little slip, there. Sorry. Did I hurt you?"

"Jesus Christ!"

"You picked a funny time to get religion, guy. Nobody's listening, I promise you."

"You won't get anything from *meeaagghh*!"

He listened to the screaming for a while and watched his puppet dance before he drew the flame away. He understood precisely what the guy was feeling, but it made no difference. This was business, all the way.

He started asking questions, and the gofer interrupted him at first, to spit obscenities, until the torch began to teach him manners. Next the dangling captive tried to bluff it out in silence, holding back the screams, but flesh was weaker than the spirit. Flesh, in fact, was sprouting blisters here and there, an abstract mural etched in bas-relief.

"I used to be a handsome guy, like you," Carboni said. "I'll bet you get a lot of action on the side."

No answer was audible beyond the weeping.

"Listen, you've already proved yourself, okay? You think that Nicky could've stuck it out this long? Forget about it. Do yourself a favor. All I'm asking is an address here and there, some names."

The flame was applied, then withdrawn. It was returned once again for emphasis.

"The ladies like you, huh? You keep this up, it's gonna be a while before you like them back. We understand each other, champ?"

A moment's hesitation came, weighing punishment against rewards.

"What is it that you want, again?"

Carboni told him patiently and listened to the answers as they were supplied. He double-checked and started over, back to front, attempting to confuse the guy on purpose, finally satisfied that he had everything he needed to proceed.

"You've been a prince," he said at last. "I knew we'd work this out between us."

"You'll let me go now?"

"I suppose it's only fair."

He killed the torch and left it on the workbench, picking up the garden shears and holding them behind his back as he returned to stand beside his dangling prisoner.

Carboni said, "I'm trusting you to take a message back to Nicky."

"Right, sure thing. You name it."

"No, on second thought, I guess it's better if we *show* him."

"Huh? I don't know what—"

He saw the shears then, and he started thrashing like a marlin on a hook, but there was no way he could beat the chains. No way at all.

"A little souvenir," Carboni said. "You get the point?"

The gofer's screaming was like music to his ears.

10

The Commerce City target was an old, two-story house on Siegal, near the Mile High Kennel Club. A normal residence by all appearances, the lawn and hedges neatly trimmed by gardeners who came each Tuesday afternoon, it betrayed no hint of what went on within. As far as neighbors were concerned, the solitary tenant was a businessman and bachelor in his early thirties, working "in communications" with a firm he never named. He liked to party—several nights a week, in fact—but he had always been discreet, and there was never any rowdiness involved. The young, attractive couples who attended social evenings at his home appeared clean-cut, soft-spoken, well-to-do.

The truth, if anyone had cared to check it out, was rather different. The "bachelor businessman," who gave his name as Edward Bates, was better known to law enforcement officers around Los Angeles as Eddie "Boots" Battaglia. The nickname dated from his reckless younger days, when he was tried, convicted and imprisoned in the stomping deaths of two Chicano hoodlums in L.A. The verdict had been set aside when witnesses began to change their stories, and a new trial freed Battaglia in time for him to take a job as an enforcer with the local Mafia.

The Mob knew talent, and a guy like Eddie Boots could have his uses when the chips were down.

These days, as Edward Bates, he worked for Nick Armato in the Denver shop. Specifically he was a talent scout and film producer, though his name had never surfaced on a Hollywood marquee. His movies did not rate reviews, beyond an occasional honorable mention in *Hustler* or *Screw*, and Eddie Boots had never been profiled on *Entertainment Tonight*.

Anonymity was a decided asset in his chosen line of work, a safety net against the risk of prosecution under state and federal statutes dealing with production, sale and transportation of pornography.

The house in Commerce City, unbeknownst to Eddie's friendly neighbors, was his studio and sound stage. Most of his productions were the standard hard-core fantasies—boy/girl, boy/boy, girl/girl—but Eddie Boots was also known to dabble in the rough trade on occasion, casting children and the odd stray animal. Authorities had noted rumors of Battaglia's involvement in the snuff-film trade, but so far there was nothing they could hang indictments on. The IRS knew sixty-odd percent of Eddie's gross went back to the Los Angeles connection, passing through Armato's hands, but proving it had stumped their best investigators up to now.

Mack Bolan, on the other hand, required no evidence that would endure through decades of appeals. *His* Bill of Rights entitled Eddie Boots to speedy execution on a charge of selling out the human race, and he had come prepared to execute that warrant on the spot.

It was a quarter past eleven when he reached the target site. A drive by showed him three cars in the driveway, two more on the street. If there were sentries, Bolan couldn't spot them in the shadows. By the time he made a circuit of the block, alert to any sign of stakeout cars, he had decided on the most direct approach.

He parked his Volvo at the curb, across the street from his intended target, taking time to double-check his armament. The powerful Beretta would be going with him in its custom armpit sheath, and Bolan wore a mini-Uzi underneath his right arm in a swivel harness that provided easy access in emergencies. His pockets held two extra magazines for each of the selected weapons, plus a number of incendiary sticks the size of ballpoint pens.

He left the car unlocked and crossed beneath a street-light, making no attempt to hide. If anybody tried to intercept him now, it simply meant that he would have to put the ball in play ahead of schedule.

On the doorstep Bolan rang the bell and waited for the better part of ninety seconds for the lookout to appear. He sized the doorman up as a gorilla: long on muscle, short on personal initiative. A decent watchdog, if you kept him fed and scratched behind his ear from time to time.

"Whozat?" he asked, all eloquence as he regarded Bolan with suspicious rodent eyes.

The Executioner responded with a bluff. "For Christ's sake, aren't you ready yet? We haven't got much time."

The watchdog looked confused.

"For what?"

"Aw, Jesus, are you telling me they didn't call? They were supposed to talk with Eddie."

"I don't know about no calls. Who *are* you?"

"I'm the guy supposed to save your ass, if I can get some help. You should've had the gear packed up by now."

"Packed up?"

"Is there a fucking echo here? The film gear, Einstein. Packed, as in we move it out before the cops drop in."

"The cops?"

He made a show of glancing at his watch. "I figure we've got ten or fifteen minutes, tops, before the black-and-whites arrive. Somebody was supposed to call an hour ago. Don't ask me what went wrong—some fuck-up, I don't know. Now, do you let me in, or do we wait for warrants?"

"Huh?"

Disgusted, Bolan shouldered past the guy without resistance, passing through a narrow entry hall to reach the living room. A young blonde in a leather teddy occupied the couch, a bored expression on her face, relaxing in between her takes.

"Where's Eddie?" Bolan asked.

The watchdog had a dazed expression on his face. "I still don't know your name," he groused.

"Forget my name, for Christ's sake. You can listen to them read it in the booking room, unless you help me get this bailout organized."

The guy caved in. "Awright, but don't blame me, okay? You say somebody should've called, but nobody did. It ain't my fault if the big boys don't know what they're doing."

Bolan followed him upstairs, then along the landing past two open doors revealing inexpensive sets. A jungle scene in one room, artificial plants and chunks of plastic foam sprayed black and gray to pass as boulders. In the other room, a prison cell motif, like something from a high-school stage production. Chains and dusty cobwebs, with a small, barred window painted on the wall.

Their destination was the last door on the left. His escort knocked, and Bolan heard a muffled curse behind the door. A moment later Eddie Boots was standing in the doorway, glaring daggers.

"What the fuck?"

His answer was a parabellum round between the eyes, the explosive impact lifting off a portion of his scalp in back and giving everyone within a dozen feet or so a piece of Eddie's mind.

The watchdog took a heartbeat to react, and it was all the time he had. The second round was placed behind one cauliflower ear, and he was down as Bolan stepped across the threshold.

Close at hand, the cameraman was frozen in his place, the scene in front of him forgotten. The assembled actors, three in number, were positioned on a rumpled bed at center stage, connected in a human daisy-chain that showed more choreography than spontaneity. All eyes were on the new arrival as he leveled his Beretta at the camera and blew the bulky lens off with a single well-placed round.

"Ten seconds!" Bolan snapped. "You've got that long to hit the bricks. This place is closed."

He snagged the cameraman en route to freedom, wedging the Beretta underneath his chin.

"I hope you've got a decent memory."

"I can't remember faces worth a damn, if that's a problem."

"Just remember *this*." he handed off a marksman's medal, making sure the weasel didn't drop it. "That's for Nicky. Tell him I was here. We're going to be seeing lots of one another."

"Right. Okay."

"Now, move your ass."

He dropped a couple of incendiaries on the set and in the hallway, one more on the stairs, another in the living room. Thick smoke was curling down the staircase by the time he reached the door. Outside, assorted cars were taking off with squealing tires, the passengers and drivers less than perfectly attired.

He waited on the porch until he saw the flames and heard them gnawing woodwork, taking hold.

It was a start.

SOME NIGHTS, you had to figure Lady Luck just wasn't running with the house. Percentages and odds were carved in stone, according to the mathematicians, but a gambler knew that sometimes you would see a run against the bank that no equations could explain. It happened, and you had to grin and bear it if you didn't want make an ugly scene and scare your paying clientele away.

So Paul Lucchese smiled and kept on smiling when he thought his face was going numb. He watched the hick from Colorado Springs lay out another thousand on the table, jiggling the dice and talking to them as though he thought they might have ears. Dumb bastard. Any second now, his luck would change, and he would see his winnings melt away.

When that began to happen, Paul Lucchese could relax. But he would keep on smiling, come what may.

Lucchese's supper club on Dartmouth Avenue, in Englewood, had been an early acquisition for Chicago when Scimone and company arrived in Denver, looking for a place to put down roots. The restaurant provided cover, a respectable facade, and Patsy had installed some tables in the back, where moneyed men were free to lose their shirts by invitation only. On the rare occasions when a patron came out winners, he was sure to talk it up among his friends, and the Scimone machine would make a killing next time.

Simple.

Hicks with money. It was perfect. Even better than Chicago, where the hard-core gamblers knew their way around.

In Denver, where the locals' closest brush with real casino action was Las Vegas or Atlantic City, back-room gambling was still a rush. The cattlemen and farmers played six nights a week—the place was dark on Sunday—and Lucchese had begun to see the same familiar faces showing up in cycles. Mr. Colorado Springs was in the middle of his third straight weekly visit, and Lucchese would have bet that he would see the guy again, same time next week.

Except that Paul Lucchese never bet on anything.

The first thing he had learned when he began to work around casinos was the folly of attempting to defeat the odds. No gambler ever born could beat the house, long-term. Forget about the crap they published in their books and magazines, describing "sure-fire systems" for defeating the casinos. It was bullshit, some guy trying to recoup his losses in another area so he could hit the tables one more time.

It was a losing proposition all around, unless you had your money riding on the house. Lucchese had his bets down on Chicago, and the Family hadn't failed him yet.

Okay, so Patsy had some rough times going down right now. So what? Lucchese had been worse, when the Spilotro brothers made their move against the capo, bucking all the odds, forgetting what they should have known to start with. *That* had been a war and no mistake, before the brothers wound up in an Indiana cornfield, beaten to a pulp but still alive when they were buried.

Paulie never bet against the house, and that was why he could afford to smile.

When things smoothed out in Denver, after Nick Armato's people and this Bolan business had been dealt with, it would be a first-class gravy train. Lucchese was anticipating a promotion, recognition of his faithful service to the outfit, once Scimone had pacified the opposition. They were tight enough—Lucchese had become adept at kissing ass as well as covering his own—and Patsy would be needing good administrators for the empire that he planned to build. In time, when they had built themselves a fortune and an army to protect it, maybe they could think about declaring independence from Chicago.

Maybe.

Once the odds began to shift.

In that case, Paulie thought, it wouldn't be like he was setting out to beat the house. Scimone would *be* the house by then, and Don Pagano would be that much older— maybe even ready for the farm. It was a thought.

But at the moment he was concentrating on the luck of Mr. Colorado Springs. A rancher with a decent line of credit; you could still mistake him for a two-bit cowboy if you didn't know his background. Chewing snuff and spitting in a paper cup between his rolls like something you'd expect to find along skid row. It took all kinds.

Four thousand riding on the table, and the bastard rolled eleven. It was his ninth straight pass, and Paulie had considered calling for another pair of dice, but it might piss the yokel off. He didn't want to lose the guy before his luck changed and the money started flowing back in the direction of the house.

Just give it time.

Lucchese shifted his attention to the other tables, covering the room from left to right. More craps, next door. A roulette wheel immediately on his right. Two blackjack tables at the far end of the room. It wasn't Vegas by a long shot, but it paid the rent with cash to spare. They picked up twenty, thirty thou a night, six nights a week, and Patsy paid him on commission, ten percent up front.

Not bad for standing on the sidelines in a monkey suit and smiling like you thought the earth was flat and didn't give a damn.

Security had been the major hang-up, going in. Once Patsy put the local vice squad wise and got them on the pad, they only had to think about Armato and his possible reaction to encroachment on the territory he regarded as his personal preserve. The place was swept for bugs and checked for bombs each afternoon before they let the dinner crowd inside, and there were always gunners on the premises in case L.A.'s ambassador tried something rash.

If all else failed—or if the Feds got wise somehow and staged a raid—there was a special exit to his right, its tunnel leading to the basement of a nearby discotheque. Before a raiding party battered down the steel connecting doors that granted access to the dining room, Lucchese's special patrons would be out of there and mingling with a crowd of boozy dancers in the disco, safely out of reach.

It was a safety hatch that he had never used and seldom thought about, secure in the thought that it was always there, just in case. All this considered, it probably wouldn't have crossed his mind tonight if the door had not blown open with a crack of sudden thunder, the concussion knocking Paulie on his ass.

He glanced up through the swirling smoke in time to see a big guy, all in black, with guns and rigs strapped everywhere, emerging from the tunnel. Paulie lost his smile at that, but the hellish ringing in his ears prevented him from understanding how a stranger could have found the tunnel, let alone employed it as an angle of attack.

Like fucking prison, right. You never thought about some crazy bastard breaking *in*.

Lucchese scrambled to his feet and hit the panic button, summoning his troops just before the man in black cut loose with a machine gun, bringing down the chandelier dead-center on the pile of cash amassed by Mr. Colorado Springs. Nobody had been hit so far, unless Paulie counted his own ruffled dignity, but Christ, with all that automatic fire—

A pair of gunners blew in from the dining room, both packing shotguns, letting go before they had a clear fix on their target. Say goodbye to Mr. Colorado Springs and one of Paulie's dealers, both men heavy as stone before they hit the floor. He shouted at the gunners, telling them to watch their aim, but they never heard him as a burst of submachine gun bullets cut them down in tandem, leaving Paulie on his own.

In retrospect his next move was a dumb-ass thing to do, but growing up along Chicago's South Side taught you *any* action—even something desperate—was a better shot than sitting on your hands.

Lucchese started for the nearest shotgun, running in a crouch, and he was close enough to feel it in his hands when the intruder fired a short precision burst and cut his legs away.

No pain at first—that must be shock in action—but Lucchese knew that he was bleeding, and his legs refused to function. Rolling over on his back, he focused on the ceiling, waiting for the guy to finish it. He wasn't ready for the looming shadow overhead, the shiny piece of metal pressed into his hand.

"Tell Patsy I was here," the big guy said. "We aren't done yet. I'll be in touch."

Lucchese didn't have a chance to answer as the tall man faded back, but then again, he didn't need to.

There was nothing left to say.

THE PARTY HAD BEEN going on since nine o'clock in Mountain View, three hours by the time he parked downrange and killed the Volvo's lights. In fact there was a get-together this time every week at Nick Armato's special party house—a sex-and-drugs extravaganza catering to the local businessmen and politicians, with the odd celebrity thrown in for color on occasion.

Bolan didn't have an inkling of the guest list going in, nor did he care. Armato's patrons checked their reputations at the door, and if a few of them should be embarrassed by exposure of their tastes, so much the better.

Still, he didn't wish them dead—not *all* of them—and Bolan chose his hardware with the care a surgeon might employ in the selection of his tools before a tricky operation. Maximum confusion, low-lethality preferred, with deadly force reserved for any opposition bearing arms.

In blacksuit Bolan wore the 93-R's shoulder rigging an an Army-issue web belt, with the Desert Eagle Magnum on his hip. The Uzi stayed behind on this run, he decided as he sorted through his grab bag, picking out the M452 "Stingball" grenades from Accuracy Systems, out of Phoenix.

Manufactured with the riot squad in mind, the Stingball strikes a happy medium between the stun grenade and standard fragmentation bombs. Its rubber casing minimizes accident damage, while the Stingball's shrapnel—scores of rubber balls the size of marbles—pack a bruising punch when they disperse at several hundred feet per second.

Bolan fit his ear plugs snugly into place—no point in taking any chance with the grenades—before he crossed the street and started his approach through darkness. Circling around in back, he scaled the redwood fence and hit a crouch inside the yard.

Armato had a sentry posted in the back beside the swimming pool, but he was concentrating on the house and wishing he could join the party when grim death stepped up behind him, squeezing off a silent parabellum round at point-blank range. Inside the house, with curtains drawn and music playing, no one heard his belly flop or watched him settle toward the bottom in a spreading pool of crimson.

Bolan tried the door in back and was surprised to find it open. Easing through, he found himself inside a modern kitchen, with back-up trays of appetizers lined up on the counter by the sink. He palmed the Desert Eagle, freed a Stingball from his belt and went to join the party.

At a glance, the sunken living room held ten or fifteen couples, all intent on coupling to the strains of jungle music thumping from a stereo on Bolan's left. Along one wall, directly opposite, the drugs had been laid out like party favors, and he watched a well-built blonde snort up two lines of prime Colombian while her companion fondled her, all smiles. A tray of marijuana joints lay close at hand, together with a candy dish of multicolored pills.

The host, presumably on hand to guarantee that no one overdosed or tried to make a naked beeline for the street, stood by impassively, the only person in the room still wearing clothes. He didn't notice Bolan in the time it took the Executioner to yank the Stingball's pin and make an underhanded pitch, allowing time to make the blast an air burst as he back-stepped, dropping to his knees.

The detonation was a shocker even with his earplugs, and the party crowd had no protection from the thunderclap or whistling rubber shot. He drew and lobbed a second Stingball in the time it took to think the action through, and he was ready for the backup gunners when they made their entrance, three guys bursting from a waiting room on Bolan's right.

They couldn't figure what was happening, and by the time they scoped it out, he had them in the Magnum's sights, unloading three hot rounds in rapid fire. The opposition melted, going down together in a sprawl of tangled arms and legs, one of the dead men squeezing off a shot in reflex, gouging plaster from the ceiling overhead.

The host was on his hands and knees, still groggy from the one-two punch provided by the Stingballs, and his paying customers were wriggling around the sunken living room like naked zombies in an open grave. The warrior left him to it and skirted the area to confront the man in charge.

He didn't know the creep and didn't want to. At the moment all he needed was a more-or-less coherent messenger. He caught the groggy mobster by his tie and hauled him upright, waiting for the bleary eyes to focus on his face and the muzzle of his .44.

"What happened?"

"Party crashers," Bolan told him, grinning through his camo warpaint. "Can you hear me?"

"Hear you?"

Close enough. He pinned a marksman's medal to the guy's lapel as if he were fastening a name tag at a convention.

"Tell Nicky I'll be looking for him. Have you got that?"

"Looking for him. Nicky. Got it."

"Perfect. Take a load off."

Bolan hit him with a solid forearm to the jaw that laid him out across the drug buffet. Retreating through the kitchen, Bolan saw the telephone and hesitated long enough to punch in 911, providing the dispatcher with an address and report of gunfire, ringing off before she asked him for his name.

The party goers should be looking for their clothes around the time the black-and-whites arrived. If there were any local biggies in the crowd, he wished them luck. All bad.

Outside, the night smelled clean and fresh, but Bolan carried the pervasive odor of munitions with him on his run back to the car. The smell was like an old, familiar friend.

Not finished yet by half, but he was on a roll.

The Denver blitz was cooking, turning up the heat, and he could only hope that it would do some good for Val. If not...

The soldier closed his mind to negatives and put his vehicle in motion, cruising like a hungry shark in search of human prey. It was a new day in the mile-high city, and a brand-new war.

11

The lockbox in Arvada, near Pomona Lake, was meant to be a secret. Even those police already on the pad were not supposed to know of its existence, since they would be almost guaranteed to disapprove. Where business was concerned, Armato and his California backers always like to play it safe. What law enforcement didn't know would never hurt them—or the Family.

The lockbox, as a concept, had been introduced by the Gambella Family in New York. Where *they* acquired the notion would be anybody's guess. The Middle East or Africa, perhaps, where life was cheap and slavery was still in vogue despite an endless stream of righteous UN resolutions calling for an end to a sale of human beings. Whatever, it had caught on quickly with a special clientele, the well-heeled sort who dare not mention their proclivities in public for the fear of being locked away in prison cells or rubber rooms.

The world was full of twisted souls, and any one of them with ready cash on hand could find nirvana in the lockbox. There would be no questions asked, no problem with disposal if a client was a little overzealous with his partner of the moment. And the "partners" came in every color of the human rainbow, every age and shape and size. They were recruited from around the country and around the world—by force, where sweet seduction failed to do the trick—and once recruited, none of them were going anywhere. A few were missed by those they left behind—their faces plastered over shopping bags and milk containers, stories profiled on the latest episode of *Unsolved Mysteries*—but none of them were ever seen again.

The lockbox, simply stated, was a gold mine. Coast to coast, there were at least a dozen such establishments, and none had ever failed to turn a profit. The Denver operation lured clients from a four-state area, and they were always satisfied. Within the past twelve months, Armato's lockbox had fulfilled the wishes of one hundred sixty-seven sadists, nineteen child molesters, two necrophiliacs and one suburban cannibal. The staff had little time for passing judgment on their paying customers. They were too busy cleaning up and filming each encounter for potential use in blackmail situations somewhere down the road.

Mack Bolan knew about the lockbox from Brognola, who in turn had gained the information from a guy who knew a guy... and so on. It was double-checked and verified, but local law enforcement had not been advised to date, since acquisition of a warrant would require Brognola to reveal his source. In lieu of burning his informant, sentencing the man to almost certain death, Hal passed the information on to Bolan, trusting in the Executioner to do what must be done.

It wouldn't be an easy in-and-out, as with the bash in Englewood. By definition the facility would be secure against both penetration and escape. The staff was armed, prepared to deal with the police or patrons who might run amok, and only proven killers would be working in the box. No conscience-ridden weaklings need apply.

It would require a special touch, and by the time he reached Pomona Lake, the soldier had his plan. A variation on a theme, with misdirection carefully applied.

He had a chance. No more, no less.

In suit and tie, without the camouflage cosmetics on his face, he was the very picture of Omega, Ace extraordinaire. The target was a sort of blockhouse, butting on the lake, and Bolan parked uprange. He wore the Uzi rig beneath his jacket, extra magazines tucked in his pockets, and he took along an olive drab satchel weighing roughly fifteen pounds.

Before initiating his approach, he used three silent parabellum rounds to cut the phone lines at the nearest pole. They might have two-way radios inside, but it was just a risk that he would have to live with. At the very least, he would delay the enemy reaction, and a blackout on the phones might help him talk his way inside.

There was a doorbell mounted on the wall, beneath a sign that cautioned No Solicitors. He held the button down for several seconds, hearing nothing from behind the soundproof door until a peephole opened to reveal one baleful eye.

"We're closed," the doorman said.

"You just reopened," Bolan told him.

"Yeah? Who says?"

He flashed the death card, waiting while the message registered.

"Nobody told us to expect you."

"Perfect. I suppose nobody told you to expect Mack Bolan, either?"

"Huh?"

"You've heard of Mack the Bastard, right? I mean, you *do* know he's in town?"

The man sounded offended now. "I heard it, sure."

"Okay, then. Nicky's shutting down until we tag him, so he can't do any kind of major damage. Word is that he knows about your operation, and they sent me out to help you batten down."

"I oughta call and check," the doorman said.

"Well, make it quick, for Christ's sake. We don't have all fucking night."

The peephole closed, and Bolan counted ninety seconds off before the glaring eye returned.

"Phone's dead," the gunner told him.

"Shit, he could be here already! Will you open up the fucking door?"

"Okay, hang on a sec."

He heard the latches being thrown and stepped across the threshold as the door was opened, the Beretta in his hand.

"You really think he's here?" the doorman asked.

"I wouldn't be surprised," the Executioner replied, and put a silent round between his eyes.

The layout was simplicity itself. A single entrance, opening directly on a north-south corridor with doors on either side. He counted twelve, the nearest on his left already open, spilling light across the no-frills concrete floor. A shadow blocked the light as Bolan took a step to meet the gunner on the threshold.

"Hey, I still can't get—"

He froze at the sight of Bolan with gun in hand and a flaccid body sprawled behind him. Groping for the weapon slung beneath his arm, the guy was never even close to saving it. A quiet chug from the Beretta, and he toppled backward in his tracks.

The regulations called for three men on a lockbox, minimum, and number three was quick enough to reach his scattergun before a parabellum double-punch sheared off the left side of his skull. Already dead, he triggered off a buckshot round that blew an empty chair away, its echo rolling up and down the hall.

Downrange a door swung open, and a balding man, his face flushed with excitement, emerged in jockey shorts and socks. The soldier pushed him back, glanced inside the Spartan cubicle and saw that whoever she had been, she wasn't breathing anymore. Bolan felt a rush of fever as the little man began to plead his case.

"It's not my fault," the scrawny monster whined. "You have to understand, I couldn't help myself."

"I'll help you," Bolan said. And shot him once, the jockeys blushing crimson as his target gave a strangled cry and hit the deck.

The other paying customers had gone, but Bolan found a youngish man in his twenties huddled in the last room on his right. The naked body was a patchwork quilt of bruises, and he cringed at Bolan's touch until survival instincts helped him recognize an ally. Bolan led him to the office, where they found his clothes rolled up inside a cardboard box, and waited while the young man dressed himself.

"Turn left outside, you'll find a Volvo on the street," Bolan said. "As soon as I get finished here, I'll drive you to the hospital."

The young man nodded silently. His still-fearful eyes were on the scattered bodies of his captors, lingering to take in every detail. Finally satisfied, he went outside, and Bolan went about his business, planting plastic charges at strategic points throughout the blockhouse, rigging detonators as he went.

Outside, he paced off fifty yards before he turned and pulled the remote-control detonator from his pocket, activating the box with the flick of a switch, mashing the solitary button with his thumb.

The lockbox lifted off in pieces as shock waves flattened the walls and hurled jagged chunks of roofing toward the sky. He turned away before the shrapnel started falling back to earth through roiling clouds of smoke and dust, and found the sole survivor waiting for him at the car.

"This won't take long," Bolan said. "We're almost there."

CARBONI HAD INVESTED in a scanner that permitted him to follow Bolan's progress, once removed, through radio reports of the police and fire departments. He had to give the bastard credit for enthusiasm, but it was impossible to cover everything at once, no matter how he tried.

So Vince decided he would help.

His first job had been dropping off the runner—minus cash and one or two of his component parts—outside a club run by Armato on Downing Street. The place was closed, but they were cleaning up inside, and Vince attracted their attention with a burst of automatic fire that blew the broad front windows out. No casualties on that one, but it did the trick, and Nicky A. would look at Bolan in a different light when he discovered where the marksman's badge was pinned.

The gofer had been helpful while he lasted, running down a list of names, addresses and unlisted numbers while Carboni jotted notes. A couple of the targets had already fallen under Bolan's guns, but there were still enough to go around.

Carboni started with an after-hours joint on Colfax, lobbing a grenade in through the basement window of a room where regulars convened to play some cards and drown their sorrows after closing time for licensed bars. He didn't wait around to do a body count, not caring who was killed or maimed. The action was its own reward, and any heat accruing from the deed would fall on Bolan's head.

Next up, he dropped in on a Glendale bookie operation, also after-hours. They were working on the daily balance sheet and sorting slips when Vincent crashed the party, taking three young punks and one old fart completely by surprise. The old man had a chance to holler "What the fuck?" before Carboni's submachine gun silenced him forever, rolling up the four of them together in a pile of lifeless meat.

He didn't bother with the money, knowing there were bigger scores ahead. Right then, he was intent on running up a score while Bolan had his own show on the road. Carboni was surprised to find how well their plans meshed in a pinch.

His fourth stop, shortly after dawn, was at a warehouse on the South Platte River, situated with water on the western flank, a rail line on the east. Three semi rigs were backed up to the loading dock when he arrived, and a crew was already at work in the first pale light of day.

The warehouse, Vincent knew, contained at least a million dollars' worth of contraband, including bootleg audiocassettes, hot furs, plus several loads of stolen video equipment. Nicky A. had contacts scattered over six or seven states, receiving goods from some and doling out to others, always turning a profit, never failing to enrich himself and those he worked for. In its time the warehouse had provided sanctuary for illicit shipments of machine guns, wetbacks, stolen cigarettes, refrigerators, TV sets—anything at all. If it bore a price tag and a hijack team could carry it away, Armato knew a buyer somewhere who was interested.

The place was slated to close immediately, but Nicky didn't know it yet. For his part, Vince had always liked a nice surprise.

He took his stuttergun, along with extra magazines, and tucked four highway flares inside his belt. The capper was a big, five-gallon can of high-test gasoline to get things started. Once the fire was rolling, Vincent figured it could get by on its own.

No lookouts.

That was stupid, any way you thought about it, with the shit that had been going down in Denver for the past few days. In Nicky's place, Carboni would have had the place well covered, but he didn't try to second-guess the strong-arm from L.A. Right then, with symptoms of fatigue becoming evident, Armato's negligence was welcome.

He met two gorillas on the loading platform and hosed them with automatic fire before they had a chance to speak or break for cover. Number three was close behind them, but he did a hasty turnaround and sprinted for the small glassed-in office to sound the alarm.

Carboni led him by a hair and caught him with a burst that pitched him over on his face, a rag doll sliding in his own blood on the concrete floor. Beyond him in the office another man was reaching for the telephone, and Vincent emptied out his magazine in one long burst that smashed the plate-glass windows, slamming one more corpse against the wall.

Reloading in a fluid, practiced motion, he retreated to the loading dock and fetched the can of gasoline. Carboni didn't have the time or energy for chasing drivers or surviving members of the warehouse crew around a maze of cartons, daring one of them to take a shot or brain him with a crowbar. He had work to do, places to go and people to kill.

He had responsibilities.

The first of which was torching Nicky A.'s investment on the spot.

Five gallons didn't stretch as far as he had hoped, but it would do. Two flares set off the lake of gasoline, and Vincent waited for the nearest cartons to erupt in flames before he tossed another flare inside the office, striking sparks atop the desk. Inside, beyond the rising wall of fire and smoke, he heard survivors shouting back and forth to one another, and he left them to it.

Vince had been there, and he had no sympathy to waste on enemies.

Armato might not lose the total inventory, but it hardly mattered now. Before the ashes cooled, there would be questions from the fire inspectors and police, requesting information on insurance, any suspects in a blatant arson case, the source of merchandise that doubtless would appear, somewhere, on master lists of stolen property.

It was enough.

Carboni had to pace himself, make certain that he stayed the course. Another stop or two, and he could take a break while Bolan tried to sort out what was happening. A rest would help, he told himself. A chance to kick back and unwind.

The lady from Wyoming might just help him out in that department if he asked her nicely. Pretty please with sugar on it, bitch.

Retreating to his car, still flushed from standing near the flames, Carboni wore a twisted, death's-head grin.

He was already looking forward to his break.

CHICAGO KNEW that drugs were Denver's leading stock-in-trade. Accordingly Scimone had taken steps to undercut Armato's profit margin, calling on connections in the South and East to flood the Rockies with a new supply, reducing short-run prices in the interest of eliminating competition. Later, once the L.A. team was safely back at home, Scimone could jack the prices up again and listen to his buyers scream. He knew damn well they couldn't do without.

A major portion of Chicago's import stock arrived un-cut in compact loads of potency too great for any human body to withstand. Scimone maintained a staff of chemists to perform the ritual adulteration, "stepping on" the coke and heroin with baking soda, powdered sugar—anything at all, in fact, to cut its purity, extend supply and guarantee that Patsy made a fair return on his investment, even at the bargain-basement price.

The operations were conducted on the fourth floor of an old brick office building near the Denver Polo Grounds. Mack Bolan had the address memorized, and after drop-ping off his passenger at Mercy Hospital, he made the run in decent time. The sun was rising, fat and red, as he ar-rived, but Bolan opted for the blacksuit anyway, combin-ing comfort and convenience with the mental edge the costume sometimes gave him over a confused opponent.

Hours yet before the straight employees started turning up for work in offices that occupied the first three floors, and Bolan didn't bother with the doors downstairs. They would be locked, he knew—perhaps with sentries posted—and he didn't plan to warn his enemies ahead of time.

In deference to common sense, Scimone had ordered that his chemists work by night, when no one but a janitor or two was on the premises. They would be cleaning up by now, prepared to sleep the day away like vampire bats, but Bolan was about to change their plans. The lab crew didn't know it yet, but they were going out of business.

With a bang.

He took the fire escape, and he was crouched outside the fourth-floor windows in about two minutes flat. His arma-ment included both the Desert Eagle and Beretta, with the mini-Uzi leading, and a representative selection of gre-nades. For safety's sake, he wore a lightweight gas mask to protect his eyes and lungs from any clouds of poison that his own explosive entry might produce.

The fourth-floor windows had been whitewashed on the inside to defeat surveillance, but it never slowed him down. The warrior pressed one ear against the glass for just a moment, picked up sounds of movement in the room beyond and wasted no more time. A frag grenade for openers, and Bolan lobbed it through the frosted pane without a target clear in mind, already flattening himself against the stairs before it blew and expelled slivered glass and whipped screams away in tatters.

Bolan followed with the Uzi, chopping down a lab technician who came reeling toward him through the smoke and drifting powder, blinded for the moment as he lurched toward death. The parabellum maulers stitched a crimson pattern on his lab coat, blowing him away before the guy knew it was done.

Another white-coat, this one running toward an exit, and Bolan helped the sprinter get there with a rising burst that swept him off his feet. Two down, and in the swirling it was difficult to say how many still were left.

A pistol shot rang out, and Bolan hit the deck, responding to the muzzle-flash as number two sliced air a yard above his head. He caught the gunner with a figure-8 that bounced him off the wall, wet traces of himself remaining as he slithered to the floor.

A second guard was shifting toward the exit, firing blindly in his haste, when one of the technicians ran across his line of fire. A hot round in the throat sent that one spinning, choking on his own life's blood, and Bolan left him to it, tracking on the gunner, firing for effect.

The Uzi's magazine was empty as he lifted off and let the twitching body fall, surrendering to gravity. He jettisoned the empty, snapped a fresh one home and rolled away before potential enemies could get a fix on his position by his muzzle-flash.

No need.

The room was silent as the echoes of his gunfire died away, and Bolan knew he was alone. His first grenade had spilled a table stocked with beakers, vials and lethal powder, kicking up the snowstorm that had momentarily concealed his entry. Now, as crystal grains of heroin began to settle on the dead, he primed a fat incendiary bomb and dropped it in the middle of the room. Retreating to the window, he ducked through before its fuse ran out, and the explosion hurled white coals of phosphorous around the loft.

A secondary blast of God-knows-what went off as Bolan reached the ground, but he was moving out, no longer interested. The thermite fire would do its work and cleanse away the filth Scimone had nurtured there. Chicago owned the building. Let it burn.

Another stop or two remaining on the hellfire trail, but first he had to stop and take the city's pulse. If anything was breaking, Hal would know about it, and he had the big Fed's local number filed away in memory.

A breather, nothing more, to weigh the impact of his strikes.

Before the Executioner went blitzing on.

12

Hal Brognola lit a fresh cigar and turned to Leo Turrin, frowning. "What's the latest count?" he asked.

"I make it twenty-seven," Leo answered, "but they can't be sure. A couple of the places burned or blew, whatever, and they won't be finished sorting through the rubble for a while."

Brognola turned back to the window of his ninth-floor room at the Downtowner Motor Inn. Directly opposite, across the flow of traffic racing east and west on Colfax Avenue, he had a clear view of the U.S. Mint. He wondered idly if it was a burn day, when they fed the old bills into an incinerator, making way for new.

"I haven't seen him on a roll like this since... when? Would it be Boston or Detroit?"

There was a shrug from Leo, and evident distraction showed on his face.

"I'm not convinced he's doing all of it."

"How's that?"

Brognola suddenly forgot about the view as he retreated to a chair and settled in across from Leo.

"It's just a hunch, so far. One thing, I *know* he didn't strafe Armato's club on Downing Street and dump that shooter—Ciccio, I think his name was—on the walk outside. The guy had been tortured, mutilated. That's not Mack."

"Okay, I'll buy that. What's the answer, then?"

"The way I see it, you've got two choices. One, the blitz is having its effect already, and Scimone is hitting back at

Nicky A. By this time, maybe both of them are making scores, with Mack caught somewhere in the middle.''

"And the second choice."

"A wild card."

"That again." Brognola made a sour face. "I hate to even think about it. Christ, we haven't got the first idea of where to start."

"It's just a hunch."

"Don't give me that. We've both been thinking it from the beginning. Striker even mentioned it in Rapid City."

"As an option."

"It looks pretty damn persuasive," Hal retorted. "I can see Armato putting on a Bolan face to hit Scimone, or maybe it's the other way around. But *both* sides? At the same damn time?"

He shook his head, disgusted, letting silence finish for him.

"Do you think he knows?"

"I couldn't tell you *what* he knows right now. He's busting targets from the shopping list we gave him, but if someone else is in the game, he may not tumble to it for a while. I don't imagine he'll be sitting down for coffee and the morning paper while he's at it."

"We should tip him off."

"I wish. You know the drill as well as I do—Striker calls us if and when he has the time. The way he's rolling now, we may not hear from him at all."

"Terrific."

"Anyway, what would you tell him? Someone *may* be out there using Bolan for a cover, but we don't know who or why. He figured that much out himself before he got here."

"We could double-check the hits he's made so far."

"I guess. And then what? Tell the locals they should skip the Executioner and put an APB out on the Invisible Man?" He slammed a fist against one knee. "God *damn*, I can't believe it's turning out like this."

"You're worried?"

"Bet your ass. There's too much riding on the line this time, and I'm still playing blindman's bluff. You never really knew Val, did you Leo?"

"Met her once," said Turrin. "At the wedding. Funny thing, you know the goddamn guy was coming from my house the night he met her? Tried to kill me in my front room, and Angelina caught him with a lucky shot. I think about it, sometimes—how it could have all been different. Figure on a minute or a half-inch, either way. He could be dead, or I would. Funny."

"I remember Vegas," Hal replied. "The night he took the Talifero brothers there at Joe the Monster's place. I had him cold. And I don't mean I was *about* to fire. I *pulled* the trigger, dead on target. Skinny little button man came out of nowhere and he threw himself in front of Striker. Took my slug and gave me one of his to grow on. You've got nothing to feel sorry for."

"It isn't that, exactly. I just *wonder* sometimes where we'd be without him."

"This is getting morbid. Striker's on a roll, and we're both acting like we're killing time before his funeral."

"You're right. Forget it, huh?"

"I'd rather not," Hal said. "Sometimes it helps to keep things in perspective. Still, we've got a couple of problems that are more important than the 'What If' game right now."

"The wild card."

"Right. And Val."

"You're thinking that if she was taken by a wild card, then the razzle-dazzle doesn't stand to shake her loose."

"How could it, if she's not with Nicky or Scimone?"

"That brings us back to motive. Someone's trusting Striker to create a war in Denver, maybe even maul both sides so badly that they're out of play."

"Because?"

"The wild card represents another Family, and his sponsors have their eye on Denver."

"Or?"

"He's got some reason why he wants to trash both sides for personal revenge."

"Suppose he's got a hard-on for the whole damn syndicate?" Brognola asked. "It wouldn't be the first time."

"No, but if he's out to bust the Mob, I can't see taking Striker on. More likely he'd be looking for a way to join the club, unless..."

"Correct. *Unless* he had a reason to hate Striker, too."

"A wiseguy?"

"Maybe, with a twist. Let's say he's had a brush with Striker in the past."

"The scars. Oh, shit."

"So, anyway, he lives to tell the story, but the boys don't want him anymore. You pick a reason—disability, whatever. Maybe looking at his face reminds the tough guys what could happen next time if they get in Striker's way. Let's say they cut him loose."

"Or try to waste him?"

"It's the standard Mafia retirement plan."

"And now he's pissed."

"To say the least."

"But if the Mob *did* try to bury him, that means he slipped away—or even took the shooters down. And now he's making moves like blowing up some guys or snatching a protected witness was a piece of cake. You have to figure that our wild card wasn't someone from accounting or the motor pool."

"I'd say that's right."

"For this to play, he would be looking at a stone mechanic."

"Right again."

"You're thinking of an Ace."

"It crossed my mind," Brognola said. "How many are there left?"

"Who knows? Except for Pat and Mike, I don't think anybody ever really knew the numbers. After Striker blew the lid off in New York, the whole thing went to hell. I still hear stories—one Ace here, a couple over there—but are they freelance? Working under the Commission? No one seems to have a handle on them anymore."

"I guess it doesn't matter," Hal replied. "If I'm on track, we're looking for an *ex*-Ace, anyway. A renegade. That makes it worse."

"It makes things tougher, that's for damn sure."

"Still, it's something. If an Ace went sour on the brotherhood and someone tried to waste him, but they blew it, that's the kind of thing you might remember."

"Scuttlebutt?"

"It's worth a try."

"Okay. I'll use the phone in my room. Leave yours free, in case. Don't hold your breath."

"I can't afford to. Gives me gas."

"I'll see you in about an hour, if you don't hear something first."

"An hour, right."

Left alone, Hal spent a moment staring out the window, studying the Mint. No matter what they did across the street that morning, it would be a burn day in the mile-high city, sure as hell.

The Executioner would see to that.

Behind him, on the nightstand, Hal Brognola's phone began to ring.

HE USED THE PAY PHONE at a service station on Louisiana Avenue. The hotel switchboard operator patched him through, and Hal picked up between the first and second rings.

"Hello?"

"Is this line clear?"

"As far as I can tell," Brognola said. "You've had a busy night."

"It isn't over yet."

"I gathered that." Hal cleared his throat. "You wouldn't have a scanner handy, would you?"

Bolan frowned. "Not with me."

"No, I didn't think so."

"What's your point?"

"This may sound funny, but I wonder if you'd let me have a rundown on the stops you've made so far."

"What is this, Hal?"

"It may be nothing, but I've got a hunch—and Leo feels the same—that someone may be operating in your shadow."

Bolan felt a prickling to his scalp, but kept the feeling to himself as he ran down the list of targets he had tagged so far. Brognola seemed to listen carefully, and Bolan wondered if he might be taking notes.

"I guess you didn't torch a warehouse on the river, then?"

"Not yet."

"No after-hours club on Colfax?"

"Negative."

"No bookie out in Glendale?"

"Nope."

"That's what I thought. Of course, we didn't have the bogus hits pinned down, per se. There was a shooting at another club Armato runs, on Downing Street. The gunner dumped a two-bit punk named Tommy Ciccio, or what was left of him. He had a marksman's medal pinned . . . well, never mind. We both knew that one wasn't yours."

"It's working," Bolan said.

"What's that?"

"The pressure. When I started, I was hoping Nicky or Scimone would be the target. Something nice and simple. Turn the heat on, they deliver Val. Or else. I've had a hinky feeling since I talked to them that maybe I was wrong."

"You spoke to *both* of them? Armato *and* Scimone?"

"This evening," Bolan said. "They both think I'm an Ace sent out by *La Commissione* to cool things off or maybe swing the balance. That's beside the point. My gut says neither one of them took Val. I'm leaning toward a wild card now. Could be he's getting ready for a confrontation."

"Funny you should mention Aces."

"Why?"

"I hashed this out with Leo—and, again, it may be nothing—but we both agree it seems to fit with what we know so far."

"I'm listening."

"We need a player with a double grudge, against the Mob *and* you. The way I see it, that boils down to a survivor of a previous encounter. Someone who's been dumped on by the syndicate—or thinks he has—for one thing or another."

"And you're thinking Aces?"

"Maybe singular. The outfit sends him in to make a tag on you, and this guy blows it. Say he takes hit—it could explain the scars—now the boys not only see him as a loser, he's not even fit for active duty."

"If he's doing everything you say he is, I'd call him fit enough."

"Agreed," Hal said, "but *they* don't think so. Maybe someone kicks him off the gravy train or tries to take him out for good. Who knows? We're looking at a guy who hates your guts, for openers, and now he has a cause to hate the Family, too. Put that together with a mind that maybe isn't wrapped too tight for starters, and you've got a lethal package."

Bolan thought about it, looking for a loophole in Brognola's logic and finding none.

"It plays," he said at last, "but I can't give you anything to go on. For a while, when Pat and Mike were still around, we used to see the Aces everywhere. I understand a few of them are still in business, but I haven't met one in a while. The ones I *did* meet used to change their names and faces like most people change their underwear."

"You're saying that it could be anyone."

"I know a few it *can't* be," Bolan answered, thinking of the Aces he had killed. "The bad news is, I couldn't even give you names for most of those."

"It stinks, I know," Brognola said, "but it's an angle. Leo's talking to his people, trying to collect intelligence. We figured that an Ace gone sour ought to rate a rumble on the grapevine. Never mind an Ace who's got a price tag on his head."

"And Val?"

"He obviously did his homework. God knows how long it would take for him to track her down. The point is, someone did."

"Let's say I buy it. If he's after personal revenge, the chances are he'll want a showdown, one-on-one. It wouldn't be the same if Nicky or Scimone got lucky."

"No, I wouldn't think so, but you never know."

"My point is that he'll need a contact to arrange the meet. Unless he's tracking me somehow and keeping tabs." He thought about it and dismissed the notion. "No, I would have seen a tail by now."

"You think Val's still alive?"

"I have to think so," Bolan said.

"This isn't what you want to hear, I know, but there's a chance that she's outlived her usefulness. I mean, she got you here—the snatch and all—but does he really need her now?"

"I don't know what he needs," the Executioner replied. "I'd have to see her dead before I'd write her off. I'm not prepared to cut Val loose on an assumption."

"No, of course not."

"If she's living, I believe he'll trot her out before we're done. It's S.O.P. in hostage situations. If she's not . . . well, then, I'll find that out before I take him."

"Watch your back."

"I always do."

"And keep in touch, huh? Leo thinks his scan should take about an hour, give or take. We might have something for you if we're lucky."

"Right."

"You had a question when you called?"

"I wanted someone else's reading on the wild card probability," he said. "You've answered that."

"Okay, then. I'll be talking to you."

"Give him time. Say ninety minutes."

"Read you."

The line went dead and Bolan cradled the receiver, mulling over Hal's suggestion of a Black Ace run amok. In Bolan's view, the wild card would have been a soldier from an outside family, lining up Chicago and Los Angeles to take each other out so someone else could sweep the broken pieces up and raise a flag in Denver. Now he thought that Hal and Leo might be on to something that made sense.

A solitary gunman *could* have tracked Val down and made the snatch. He *could* tie up Armato and Scimone with random hits, impersonating Bolan's style. The proof was Bolan's own survival, one man taking on the syndicate and scoring major goals. It had been done before and could be done again.

The problem, this time, was that someone wanted Bolan in the middle of the play, like fresh meat in a sandwich. His opponent—Ace or otherwise—was counting on the Executioner to keep things boiling in the Denver pot until an opportunity came up for him to step on Bolan like an insect.

Personally.

Nothing else made any sense at all.

It gave the warrior hope, because a personal solution meant his enemy would need a hole card—namely, Val. If Mr. X was counting on the syndicate to finish Bolan, it would make no difference whether Val survived or not. She would have served her purpose as a lure, and common sense would dictate that she be destroyed before she could become a liability.

A one-on-one approach made all the difference in the world.

Without the woman, Bolan's wild-card opposition had no leverage. Bolan would be free to drop the game and walk away at any time without a backward glance. He wouldn't be in Denver were it not for Val, and if he thought that she was dead, there would have been no reason to remain.

Except revenge.

Armato and Scimone might not have fingered Val for her abductor, but their troops were handy, and he would not miss an opportunity to thin the herd. If anything, in light of Hal's suggestion for the wild-card option, his Denver blitz was even more imperative. Only by exposure through his random strikes could Bolan give the unknown enemy an opportunity for contact, and only by emerging from the shadows to continue the attack would he have any chance at all of finding Val.

That said, the soldier's choice came down to no damn choice at all.

13

The target was a pool hall east of Harvey Park, on Evans Avenue. It wasn't much to look at, but the dozen tables paid for overhead and then some, with the hangout serving as an unofficial home away from home for street kids, dropouts, teenage gangsters and the other flotsam of a mostly non-white neighborhood. The manager was sixty-five years old and built like Mama Cass. His posted rules—against profanity and fighting, betting on the games or spitting on the floor—were generally ignored, but while the register kept making music, no one seemed to care.

The pool hall's manager was not its owner. Nick Armato had acquired the property a short time after moving east from California, when he noticed that the local numbers racket was controlled by blacks. Before the month was out, Armato had begun to seek a "balance" in the name of equal opportunity, presenting numbers bankers with a list of options: join the winning team, get out of town or die. To make it stick and save himself the hassle of a race war, Nicky chose the toughest gang around—the Warlords—and immediately put its leaders on the payroll. Almost overnight the opposition had begun to fade.

Upstairs, above the pool hall, Nicky's largest numbers bank and counting house enjoyed the dual protection of the Warlords and a team of hardmen from the L.A. Family. When drunks or nosy players tried to breach the inner sanctum, they were turned away by punks downstairs. The force employed to turn them back depended on the individual's belligerence, but few saw fit to tangle with the Warlords over anything so trivial. In theory, if a stranger reached the upper floor without a pass from Nicky A. or one of his lieutenants, the gorillas standing watch would make him sorry he was ever born.

The Executioner had chosen Nicky's bank deliberately, led by the desire to hit the mobster where he lived. The neighborhood would make it tougher, but he thought the morning hour should compensate enough to make it even. At the very least, he should not have a problem with civilians getting in his line of fire.

He parked the Volvo out in front, beside a meter with an out of order tag, and tried the door. It opened to his touch and Bolan stepped inside, his nostrils flaring at the pent-up reek of perspiration, smoke and beer gone flat. He wondered if they ever gave the place an airing and decided it was overdue.

The rotund manager—still here, or just arriving—glanced at Bolan from behind the register and turned away. He was accustomed to receiving strangers dressed in flashy suits, all hours of the day and night, without a second thought. Their business didn't overlap with his, and he had reached the age of sixty-five by treading lines of careful circumspection with a tightrope walker's skill.

The Warlords were a different story. Three of them were lounging near the stairs, one sucking on a beer, the others smoking, staring hard at Bolan from the moment that he crossed the threshold. White skin set their teeth on edge, but they had learned to tolerate the interlopers for a price. They didn't recognize this honky, though, and suit or not, somebody should have called ahead.

The three were on their feet before he reached their table, fanning out to block his path. The stairs lay just beyond, and it was clear that he would have to pass the keepers of the gate before he reached his goal.

"Hey, white meat, what it is?"

The tallest of the Warlords had a gold-capped tooth in front. It matched his nose ring and the chains around his neck. Like his companions, he wore faded denim with the sleeves hacked off his jacket, sporting pins and badges that would have significance for members of the gang. The leader wore a black beret with a skull-and-crossbones badge; his sidekicks wrapped their heads in red bandannas.

"It looks like I'm about to go upstairs," said Bolan, letting ice show through his smile.

"You better think again, man. No one makes the trip without an invitation."

"Really?"

"Tha's the rule."

The smile remained in place as Bolan said, "I think I've got one here. Hold on a second, will you?"

Bolan was fishing in his pockets as the leader sneered and said, "Don't shuck me, whitey." Stepping closer as his right hand came out empty, the Executioner snapped in a vicious straight-arm with the fingers curled, his rigid palm impacting on the young man's nose.

It might have been a lethal blow, but wasn't. Bolan pulled his punch enough to spare the hoodlum's life, but he was out of it before he hit the floor, his two companions startled but recovering in time.

Almost in time.

The one on Bolan's right produced a switchblade, lunging toward his mark with more aggressive zeal than foresight. Bolan sidestepped, took the thug's wrist and wrung it like a dishrag, putting sudden leverage on the elbow. When it gave, the snap distinctly audible, his adversary vomited at Bolan's feet and then collapsed, facedown, to blot it with his colors.

Number three had found himself a pool cue by the time he came at Bolan, swinging overhand. The soldier went inside the blow, took some of it across his shoulder, fingers closing on the gangster's throat and privates simultaneously. Bolan used his legs for leverage, a twisting motion like a discus thrower, lifting his opponent off the floor in time to slam his skull against the nearest wall.

Three up, three down.

He took the time to smooth his rumpled jacket, climbed the narrow flight of stairs and banged his fist against the wooden door marked Private. The response was instantaneous, and a hard face filled up the four-inch gap as it was opened on a safety chain.

"You ready?" Bolan snapped before the guard had time to think.

"Say what?"

"I'm here to make the pickup," Bolan said, exaggerating his pronunciation as one might when speaking to an idiot. "Let's snap it up, okay?"

"What pickup? Who the hell are you?"

He flashed the ace just long enough to make the gunner blink.

"That's who I am. You got a problem with it?"

The sentry hesitated, afraid to push too far, but still uneasy with the break in his routine.

"They let you pass downstairs?"

"We had a little heart-to-heart. Your boys don't feel so well right now."

"Hang on a second."

Bolan waited while the door was closed and the chain unfastened, then brushed past the gunner to confront the man in charge.

"What's going on here, may I ask?"

The banker was a shrimp with a receding hairline and a pair of spectacles. He was trying to look as though he was in command, but his features reflected a nervous uncertainty.

"Pickup time," the Executioner replied. "All set to go?"

"I'm sure I don't know what you mean."

"You had a call," he bluffed. "We're closing down till further notice. Too much heat, with all the shit that's going down."

"There's been no call," the banker told him, frowning like a man who's lost his last, best friend.

"No call? Well, Jesus Christ! We got a tip the Feds are rolling in about—" he checked his watch "—five minutes down the road. Somebody was supposed to call you so you'd have the inventory set to roll."

"There's been no call." The little guy was sweating now.

"Okay, here's what you do. You don't believe me, drop a dime, but make it snappy. I've allowed myself three minutes, and I wasted one of those downstairs with the Three Stooges. Another hundred twenty seconds, and I'm out of here. If I go empty-handed and the Feds pick up this swag, I guarantee you Nicky's gonna fry somebody's ass."

The banker took a shot at imitating a chameleon, changing colors—red to purple, purple fading into bloodless white—before the warrior finished. With a strangled curse, he scuttled off to round his people up, and Bolan watched them stuffing greenbacks into luggage they had standing by.

"Forget the coins," he told them from the sidelines. "Hercules stayed home today."

Two bags of cash—he didn't even bother counting—and the crew was working on a third when Bolan made his move.

"We're out of time," he snapped. "I'll take this load— the rest of you work out a place to meet and carry what you can. I'd say you've got about two minutes left before the Feds drop by."

A sentry held the door, two others stepping up to serve as Bolan's escort, but he warned them off. "I've got it covered, boys. You stick around and make sure none of what I'm leaving gets misplaced, you follow me? And take a thou each for yourselves, on me. We'll call it hazard pay."

"Yes, sir!"

He left them to it, clomping down the stairs with two bags full of cash, a pleasant weight on either side. The Warlords didn't notice him on the return trip, and he scarcely noticed them.

His eyes were on the new arrival standing in the doorway. Dressed in grays and black, a turtleneck beneath his charcoal jacket, snap-brim hat pulled low about a face that had been deeply scarred by fire.

The face.

No time to register as Bolan checked the new guy's hands. The right was incomplete somehow, but in a flash he saw the left made up for it, a stubby Ingram submachine gun sprouting from the fist.

He dropped the bags of cash and broke for cover, sliding in behind the nearest billiard table as the world exploded overhead.

CARBONI PICKED the numbers bank because it was a natural, a chance to sting Armato and replenish his own war chest in the process. Living on the road wasn't an inexpensive proposition, and if everything went smoothly, he would need some ready cash to fund his getaway. He knew the risks involved and came prepared to deal with any opposition that he might encounter.

But he didn't count on Mack the Bastard being there to greet him.

Just across the threshold, Vince had frozen at the sight of three young black men laid out on the floor. Immediately to his right, a fat old man was cowering behind the register and trying hard to make himself invisible. Carboni didn't bother shooting him, convinced it would have been a waste of ammunition.

Moving toward the stairs, he heard the heavy footsteps coming down. At first he just saw feet, then legs and matching luggage. Next, a torso, and his stomach had begun its barrel roll when Vince beheld the face. It was a living image from his nightmares. Smug, self-satisfied.

He read surprise in Bolan's glance, but nothing close to recognition as they faced each other at a range of forty feet. Carboni had not banked on Bolan knowing him—their single meeting had been brief, a skirmish in the darkness—but he made the Executioner on sight. A heartbeat's hesitation, and Vince knew he had to move.

No planning, no rehearsal. It was nothing like he'd hoped, but golden opportunities don't drip in every day. He thrust the Ingram out and squeezed the trigger in smooth reflex motion, tracking as his target made a dive for cover.

Parabellum rounds chewed up a billiard table's felt and woodwork, peppering the wall, but as the magazine ran out Carboni knew that he had missed.

He dumped the clip and drew another with his lobster claw, reloading swiftly. Bolan took advantage of the momentary lull to squeeze off two quick rounds, and Vincent answered with a burst that went in high and wide, a product of excitement rather than his normal cool reserve.

Now he was a step behind. He bolted for the exit as his adversary fired another round, the bullet smashing glass on Vincent's right. He almost stumbled, making for his car a half-block down, and at a glance he knew the Volvo would be Bolan's car. He was about to let the engine have a burst when Bolan triggered two rounds through the window, one slug plucking at the sleeve of Vince's jacket.

He fired back through the window, plate glass coming down in jagged sheets, and then his legs took over, pumping as he sprinted for his car, his feverish thoughts keeping pace with his feet: So slick, you bastard, but we're not done yet. Not by a long shot.

Peeling out before his door was closed, Carboni spent the first two blocks assessing damage. He was halfway through the third before he realized he had a tail.

Then Vincent knew he hadn't lost the bastard, after all.

THE DIVE BECAME A ROLL on impact, freeing Bolan's weapon, bringing the Beretta to his hand. Above him automatic fire swept back and forth across the table, scattering a rack of balls and turning some of them to powder where they sat.

He knew the Ingram's awesome rate of fire, its magazine capacity, and he was ready when the scar-faced gunner broke off to reload. No time to aim, but Bolan's two quick rounds were close enough to make his adversary dance. He got a third shot off before his target cleared the threshold, two more through the window as the guy turned right along the sidewalk. Brisk return fire drove him back to cover for a moment, and the man was gone.

Almost.

The soldier scooped up one bag full of money—no point in forgetting why he came—and followed at a run. He saw the Chevrolet peel out, downrange. Deciding not to risk a shot and chance random ricochets into shops along the streets, he tossed the suitcase in the Volvo, slid behind the wheel and squealed away in hot pursuit.

They traveled east on Evans, Bolan closing up the gap until his quarry realized he had a tail. The Chevy showed its spirit then, unlimbering a beefed-up power plant and topping sixty-five before they reached the greenery of Harvey Park.

As Bolan drove, he tried to place the twisted countenance and draw a name from memory, but nothing came. For just an instant in the pool hall, there had been a hint of grim familiarity, but it had been erased as automatic fire erupted in his face and instinct took control.

But name or not, he knew that he was following the wild card—shiny scars, a burn. But it still told him nothing.

Weaving in and out of the morning traffic, leaning on his horn at intersections, Bolan's prey crossed Lowell, King and Knox. He plowed directly through the north-south flow on Federal, narrowly escaping contact with a bus, and Bolan swung around the silver giant, tires protesting the abuse.

No room to try a shot as they crossed Bryant, Zuni and Vallejo, rolling east. The traffic slowed him down, but he wasn't prepared to sacrifice a hapless driver or pedestrian in haste. Besides, he needed both hands on the wheel as cars and trucks loomed out of side streets, heedless of the chase in progress, braking late or not at all.

The Volvo had a few new dings and creases—he would have to ditch it, after all—before his quarry got to Broadway, barreling across on red. Cross-traffic fishtailed, rubber burning, and from where he sat the Executioner could see a taxi climb the bumper of a black-and-white, the stunned patrolmen rocking in their seats. A biker slid his Honda down in front of Bolan, and the Volvo's brakes were barely tight enough to save it as Bolan veered left between two vehicles and rolled through an alley parallel to Broadway.

His quarry was lost.

He didn't have a prayer of overtaking his assailant now, no matter how he tried. He reached Asbury Avenue and waited for an opening in traffic, listening to sirens as the traffic officers responded to a call on the collision. If he took his time and played it cool, there would be nothing to connect him with the crash.

And if his quarry had eluded him, at least he had a picture of the gunner's face indelibly recorded in his memory.

Another pang of déjà vu invaded Bolan's consciousness, but there was nothing he could make of it. The face—if it was one that he had ever known—had been resculpted by the flames and plastic surgeons, stretched and twisted into something like a ghoulish caricature of itself. If he had time, it might be possible to postulate and reconstruct a face from memory, but it would only be a kind of guesswork. He would never know for sure until he tracked the gunner down.

The other possibility was the Fed. Brognola had informed him that the search would take an hour. They were coming up on that as Bolan found himself a service station, parked near the pay phone and climbed out to stretch his legs and check the damage to his car.

It would survive, but it would have to go.

He set his mind: first things first.

A name to tell him who had kidnapped Val. With any luck, a face to match the name. That done, he merely had to find one man—one cunning man—among the several hundred thousand residents of Denver and its suburbs.

Easy, right.

Like dying.

Bolan palmed a coin and headed for the telephone.

14

The meeting had been set for noon at an amusement park beside Lake Rhoda on the eastern side of Denver. Bolan used the intervening time to buy himself a Chrysler four-door, shifting his equipment to the newer car and dropping off the Volvo in an underground garage where it would not attract undue attention for a day or two at least.

As he entered the amusement park, proceeding toward the midway, Bolan's mind was not on fun and games. Brognola had been cryptic on the telephone, insisting on a face-to-face when he delivered the intelligence that Leo had collected from his contacts in the syndicate. It wasn't like Hal to be coy, and Bolan had to figure it was serious.

Like life and death.

He moved along the midway, dry grass crunching underfoot, the power cables serving booths and rides strung out around him like a tangled nest of giant snakes. The rides were mostly running empty, since the park had just been open for an hour. Barkers tried to interest Bolan in their wars—a funhouse, freak shows or a chance to win a goldfish at the coin toss—but he passed them by, proceeding to the shooting gallery.

The weasel in the booth was polishing a light, pump-action .22 when Bolan stepped up to the firing line. He seemed surprised to have a customer.

"That's five shots for a quarter, sport."

"I'll take a dollar's worth."

"I like your confidence."

Behind the weasel, metal silhouettes of animals ran back and forth on hidden tracks, arranged in tiers with ducks below and cartoon grizzlies at the top. His first shot told him that the rifle's sights were bent—no doubt deliberately—and Bolan compensated, scoring nineteen hits with twenty rounds.

"Your lucky day," the carny said without enthusiasm. "For your prize you've got a choice of anything along the first or second shelves."

The Executioner ignored him, smiling as he settled on a giant panda, more or less life-size.

"Why not the bear?" he asked.

"For that you have to score with twenty shots," the barker told him, adding, "it's the rules."

"Okay, I'll take another dollar's worth."

"Why not? I got a honey of a gun right here."

"I'll stick with this one," Bolan said. "Why don't you load it up."

The guy was thinking of an argument, but one more look at Bolan changed his mind. "Why not?"

This time he concentrated on the grizzlies, picturing a scarred and twisted face as he dropped twenty in a row.

"Nice shooting," Hal Brognola said from behind him.

At his other elbow Leo Turrin said, "You must get lots of practice."

Bolan forced a smile. "I try to keep in shape." He turned to the barker. "The bear?"

Reluctantly the man handed him his prize, and Bolan passed it to Brognola. "With my compliments," he said as Hal began to wrestle with the giant toy, discovering that there was no convenient way to tuck a panda underneath one arm.

"Let's take a walk," the big Fed grumbled, hefting his inert companion like a heavy sack of groceries.

"I assume you didn't call me all the way out here to say you came up empty."

"Oh, we got a name, all right," Leo said, falling into step on Bolan's left. "The question is, do you believe in second comings?"

"What's the name? I'll let you know what I believe."

"The name's Carboni, Sarge."

The words hit Bolan like a rabbit punch below the ribs. "You're sure?"

"No way," Hal answered, "but the information jibes with what we've seen so far."

The name took Bolan back to Baltimore, to his campaign against Don Carlo Nazarione. Carboni had been tracking Bolan well before the play in Maryland, he later realized. Two months before, a narrow miss in Oregon had been the Ace's first attempt, and Vince from Philly never let things rest while his opponent had the lead. Their showdown was precipitated by a hostage situation on a farm outside of Baltimore, with Carboni using every trick at his disposal to destroy the Executioner. One gag had backfired, though—quite literally—and the soldier's final glimpse of Ace Carboni was of a figure bobbing in a wheat field, trapped by flames he lit himself.

"Carboni's dead."

"We thought so, too. The wiseguys disagree."

Bolan was quiet as he remembered that face again, those scars. If the man *had* survived—what a motive of hate and revenge.... "I'm listening."

The story came from Leo, Hal assisting on the odds and ends from Washington while he continued grappling with the panda.

"You thought Carboni bought it on the farm. We thought so, too. But now it turns out someone found him on the highway and they drove him to a country doctor. God knows how he managed to survive the trip, but when they got him to the burn ward, he had sense enough to give a phony name and let them have a number that connected with his link to *La Commissione*. From there the Mob took over—specialists, a private nurse, the whole nine yards. It had to be a bitch, but over time Carboni pulled himself together, more or less."

"Except?"

" 'Except' is right. It seems the Mob was spending so much money on this guy because he'd turned himself into the local Bolan expert. He was scoping out your past for weeks before the thing in Oregon, and that one pissed him off so badly that he got a little reckless at your one-on-one in Baltimore."

"Okay. The way I hear it, the Commission figured they could still use Vincent's brain, but no one really thought he'd make it back to active duty. Something with a hand, some fingers gone or something, and the scars would be a giveaway for any witnesses."

"Go on."

"Well, anyway, Carboni had a different slant on things. He couldn't feature sitting back and telling someone how to take you out—he had to do the job himself. The big boys warned him off, but someone let him have a few small contracts on the side to see if he could function. Call them warm-ups. He was getting ready for the main event, and there was no way anyone could talk him out of it. He was obsessed with getting back on line and tracking you, at any cost. A few months down the road, the brass decided he was crazy and they farmed a contract out."

"It didn't take," said Bolan, confident of the response.

"You got that right. According to the scuttlebutt, at least four guys have tried to take him, and he smoked them all. Some say it's better than a dozen, but you know the way these stories get inflated as they make the rounds. Whatever, Vince Carboni is a fixture on the outfit's drop-dead list, and it's a safe assumption that he's not amused."

"The homework led him back to Val?"

"We're pretty sure," Hal answered. "It appears that someone has been following a paper-trail—inquiries on a marriage license, things like that—and I'd lay odds it was Carboni."

"Contacts?"

"No one who'll admit it," Leo said, "but we suspect that he's been cashing in old markers on the sly. The outfit has him down for scores in Cleveland and Detroit, where cash was taken. As it is, the losers have to stand in line to take their shot, and nobody can pin the bastard down."

"They haven't tied him in with Denver?"

"Not so far. *You're* supposedly raising all this hell, re-member? Vincent may be crazy, but the outfit hasn't pegged him as a Bolan imitator."

"Maybe someone ought to whisper in their ear."

"You think so?"

"I'll consider it."

He knew the risks involved if members of the syndicate began to stalk Carboni in the mile-high city. Gunners sent to bag the rogue Black Ace at any cost wouldn't concern themselves with Val's survival, and they might decide to kill her as a witness if and when they tracked Carboni to his lair. The flip side lay in Bolan's knowledge that the Mafia would have a better chance of tracking Vincent down—if nothing else, because of numbers, contacts on the street—while Bo-lan might pursue his man for weeks without another sight-ing in the flesh.

The question was, if the mob was so efficient, why was Vince Carboni still alive?

The answer to that was easy. Because they didn't know precisely where to look, for starters, and the syndicate had other problems on its hands these days. With prosecutions and indictments pouring in on every side, a problem out of sight became a problem out of mind. Carboni would be killed if he was found, but in the meantime, while he man-aged to conceal himself, the Mafia had other fish to fry.

Like Bolan, right.

"I don't suppose you've talked to any of Carboni's doctors?"

"We're working on it, but it's bound to take some time. You've got the basic doctor-patient confidentiality, plus we have to figure some of them are working for the Mob, at least part-time."

"I'm looking at Carboni's state of mind."

Brognola peered around the panda. "My thought, too. When Leo mentioned crazy, I got on the line to Quantico. The Bureau has a shrink on tap who works with VICAP—Violent Criminal Apprehension Program—and Behavioral Sciences, running down serial killers and geeks like that. We had some words before you called."

"Go on."

"Okay, but bear in mind it's hypothetical. He figures that Carboni started out as what we used to call a psychopath—no conscience, antisocial, cold and calculating, basically manipulative. All the good stuff. That is *not* psychotic, by the way, which indicates delusions and a loss of contact with reality. The psychopath knows what he's doing all the time—the problem is, he doesn't give a shit."

"I'm with you so far," Bolan said.

"Anyway, the doc says these types normally have egos that would make Napoleon look modest," Hal continued. "Figure someone like Carboni has to use a yardstick for his hat size, if you follow me. But when the wiseguys sent him after you, the doc thinks maybe—*maybe*—Vincent thought he'd found his equal, or at least a fitting challenge. Either way, we *know* he came away from Baltimore with a fixation on revenge. You slipped away from him in Oregon, and then you fried his ass the second time around. Or worse, you made him do it to himself. Throw in the shock of major burns—potential damage to the brain from injuries and lack of oxygen—and the fact that now his bosom pals have turned against him. Any way you look at it, the guy's a candidate for raving paranoia."

"But he functions?"

"Like a charm, within the scope of his appointed mission. That's the kicker with a psychopath. He isn't hearing voices, Striker. God won't tell him what to do or when to call it off. He isn't seeing men from Mars or talking to himself in public. Quantico says chances are he's more efficient now, aside from any physical debilitation, than he was before."

"The paranoia?"

"What the hell? The world *is* out to get him, when you think about it. Law enforcement, you, the syndicate—it makes *me* paranoid, just standing here."

"And where does that leave Val?"

Brognola glanced away, diverting his attention to the panda in his arms. "I didn't have the time to run that down at any length," he said.

"I'll run with what you've got."

"All right. The best the doc could say was it's a fifty-fifty proposition. She means nothing to Carboni as a person, but he needed her—or someone like her—for a lure. That's why he took her out of Sheridan alive . . . we hope."

"I'm interested in what comes next."

"It could go either way. If he could rig a confrontation, face-to-face, she might be useful. Recreate the hostage situation where you beat him once before, that kind of thing. Turn that around, and if Carboni sees he doesn't have a chance to play High Noon, then Val's no more than excess baggage. He could dump her anytime and never bat an eye."

"She could be dead already."

"It's a possibility."

"And we could never tell."

"Without Carboni it would take a miracle."

"That says it all," the Executioner replied. "Without a body to confirm, I have to act on the assumption that she's still alive. If I go any other route, I'm throwing her away."

"Your call," Brognola said. "I don't know how you'll find him, either way."

"I've seen him once already," Bolan said.

"How's that?"

He briefed them on the details of his confrontation with Carboni at the numbers bank, the chase that followed and his quarry's lucky break on Broadway.

"It was him? You're sure?"

"What's sure? The face—what's left of it—was more or less familiar, but I couldn't place it. Naturally I wasn't thinking resurrection at the time. Unless you've got another candidate in mind, I'm ready to confirm the sight-ing."

"Meaning what? You lost the guy."

"He won't stay lost for long. I don't believe Carboni set this whole thing up to watch it from a ringside seat. He's letting me mop up the Families—or helping me, from what you say—but he'll be waiting at the other end to take me down himself."

"Suppose he tried already? One more fumble, and he might flip out."

The soldier shook his head. "I'm betting that the bank was a coincidence. We're both out making hits and choosing targets from a limited supply. It stands to reason that our paths would cross at some point. If I'm right, he won't consider this a setback. Looking at it from another angle, it might even stroke his ego. This time, *he* gave *me* the slip."

"That still leaves future contact unresolved," said Hal. "You can't exactly take out an ad in the *Denver Post*."

"I shouldn't have to. If he has half the brain you say, Carboni will be following the action right along. Don't ask me how—an inside man, surveillance, something—but I have to figure that he won't be overlooking any major moves."

"A full-scale rumble. Nicky and Scimone. The main event."

"And if he shows?"

"I have to try and flush him. Chances are he won't be traveling with Val. He'll have her stashed somewhere, if she's alive. Next time I get him in my sights, I have to stick until he leads me home."

"You really like to gamble, don't you?"

"Have I got a choice?"

To that there was no answer.

"There you are, then."

"Is there anything that we can do to help?"

"You've done it, thanks."

"Logistics, maybe?"

"You can try to keep your people clear. A four-way fire-fight doesn't leave a lot of room for choreography."

"Okay. There isn't much that I can do about the locals."

Bolan shrugged. "If things work out, I should be tracking Vince before they roll the riot squad. He's all I want. The uniforms are welcome to Armato and Scimone, if they can handle it."

"I don't know how they stand on combat training, but my hunch is that we'll see."

"I guess. Well, if there's nothing else . . ."

"I wish there was."

"Okay. Sit tight, and maybe I'll be talking to you."

"Maybe?"

"I'm no good at telling fortunes, Hal."

He left them on the midway, Leo and Brognola and the giant panda, moving through the growing crowd to reach the parking lot. With every step he took, the Executioner was thinking of Carboni in the flames, the hatred he must feel inside for Bolan and the syndicate, the world at large.

He understood his adversary now, but he wasn't about to sympathize.

If Val was harmed, the renegade Black Ace would have another date with hellfire waiting, and he would not walk away from this one. Not if Bolan had a chance to call the shots.

Whichever way it played, the Executioner was primed to strike a spark in Denver and ignite the cleansing fire.

15

Val knew that time had passed because she had slept, despite her fear, and woke up hungry. Whether it was hours or days, she couldn't tell. For a while she had tried to count the minutes, ticking off "one thousand one, one thousand two" inside her head, but it had quickly proved to be a fruitless and infuriating exercise. When all else failed, she paced the two small rooms and prayed that she would find a secret passage overlooked by her abductors. All in vain.

The house was silent now except for distant street sounds, as it had been during most of her incarceration. Once, at some point that was surely hours earlier, a car had stopped outside. She heard doors opening and closing at a distance, followed by a murmuring of voices she couldn't identify or understand. A short time later, tortured screams began to echo through the furnace ducts beneath her feet, continuing until she shut herself inside the bathroom, hands pressed tight against her ears to drown them out.

So insulated, Val wasn't precisely sure of when the screaming stopped or when her captor left the house again. She might have huddled in the shower-bath for hours, but she thought it had been less. Perhaps an hour at most. In any case the house was quiet when she dared to move her hands. No screams, no voices. Nothing but the sound of Val's own beating heart to keep her company.

And hunger.

It wasn't necessarily true, she found, that fear destroyed one's appetite. Her stomach growled, reminding Valentina that she had not eaten in—how long? Too long. By an estimate she would have missed at least two meals. It felt like four or five.

The hunger was encouraging in one respect. The drugs had made her nauseous, but the feeling had retreated and finally disappeared, leaving only a persistent headache and the bruising at her elbow to remind her of the hypodermic needle. Lately, when she dozed, Val woke up with her memory intact, clearheaded, knowing where she was.

Or more precisely, where she *wasn't*.

She was not at home with Jack, and thinking of him revived her feelings of anxiety. She knew that he was wounded, but she didn't know how badly. He might lie unconscious in the house for days, unless—

She stopped herself. Again she thought of Bolan, knowing he was part of it somehow. Had her abductors been in touch with him? Could anyone make contact with him, short of putting up a billboard on the interstate and hoping Bolan passed that way? What use was Val to anyone, without a pipeline to the Executioner? Would Bolan come, in any case?

So many questions, but the last one was the only query Val could answer categorically. If Mack knew she was threatened—if he even thought she was in danger—he would try to help her. Sacrifice himself, if need be, to release Val from her cage. She knew that as well as she knew anything on earth, and it was tearing her apart.

Her mind rebelled against the thought of being used to trap the man whom she had loved. *Still* loved, in so many ways. If only they had never met, or she had died in Boston when the Mafia had tried to use her once before. She would have missed so much, the love and happiness she found with Jack and Johnny, but she hated the thought of having no control, of being used to engineer the downfall of somebody she treasured deeply.

Val shook herself to break the morbid train of thought. Her stomach growled again, but there was nothing she could do about the nagging hunger. On the other hand, she felt unclean, and there was definitely something she could do to remedy *that* problem.

Listening for several moments, straining to detect the slightest sound, she satisfied herself that she was alone. A hasty shower wouldn't hurt. In fact her captor had apparently supplied the bathroom with her basic needs in mind. The soap and towels had not been left by accident.

A quick one, then, with no one to disturb her. Taking extra care, she closed the bathroom door, imagining that it might further mute the shower's noise. Of course, the sound of running water would be audible throughout the house— the *empty* house—but instinct goaded her to take the few precautions that she could.

She turned the shower on and spent a moment on the temperature, adjusting it until the water was as hot as she could stand. Val caught a tacky whiff of perspiration as she peeled her flannel nightgown off, the odor wrinkling her nose. She thought of rinsing out the garment while she had the shower on, but in the absence of a change of clothes she let it go. The smell was one thing; being naked in a cage was something else.

Val blanked her mind to danger as she stepped inside the shower, flinching as the steaming spray made contact with her flesh. A moment to adapt, and then she let the shower melt her tension, washing it away. She raised her face, eyes closed, and felt the thick hair plastered to her skull. Val thought she would survive this once without shampoo.

She pivoted to let the water drum against her back, soothing her muscles, before she took the soap in hand and started working up a lather on her skin. In spite of everything it felt so good that Val decided she would take a moment to enjoy the fact of being clean again. The simple pleasures.

She soaped herself all over twice to kill the odor of captivity. If she were home, she might ask Jack to scrub her back. He always made believe that he was busy, but he never failed to join her when she called him. Val could almost feel his hands, all businesslike at first, until they slipped around in front of her to cup her breasts or slid between her thighs.

Her eyes snapped open as she caught herself. The fantasy was out of place in these surroundings, when she didn't know if she would ever hear Jack's voice or feel his soothing hands again. Impulsively she spun the shower knob and felt the shock of icy water pelting down. It made her shiver, but she stood her ground, her nipples puckered from the cold and goose bumps rising on her flesh.

It worked. Another miracle.

She turned the shower off and pulled a giant bath towel from the rack, beginning with her hair and working down her body to her legs and feet. Before she finished, she was tingling from head to toe, her skin a rosy color from the combination of the shower and the chafing terry cloth. It seemed a shame to put the clammy nightgown on again, but she was left without a choice.

Val used her fingers as a comb to work the major snarls and tangles from her hair, deciding that a style was hopeless. She would let it dry the way it was, and if her jailers didn't like it, they could damn well let her go.

She stepped across the bedroom threshold and instantly recoiled from the man who stood before her, smiling through a mask of scars.

"You took your own sweet time," he said, "but it was worth it."

COMING OFF THE CHASE, Carboni felt a heady mixture of emotions, anger and elation battling for the upper hand. It made him furious that Bolan had surprised him, that he had been forced to run away, but on the other hand he had survived, eluding his pursuer in a chase that could have ended in disaster.

It was sheer coincidence, Vince told himself, that he had stumbled onto Bolan at the counting house. Their orbits were designed to intersect—his scheme depended on it—and he should have been prepared for the encounter when it came. The money was a secondary problem—there was always more where that came from—but he would have to check his negligence before it got him killed.

Next time Bolan would not hesitate. Carboni would be forced to concentrate on every move he made from that point on until the game was over and he had his prize in hand.

The bastard's head would do.

Retreating toward his safehouse by the stockyards, Vincent wondered if the Executioner had recognized his face. Would anyone, without an introduction? It was possible, of course, but it would ruin the surprise Carboni had been planning all these months.

On second thought, he told himself, it might be better if the soldier *did* know who was stalking him. If Bolan thought Carboni had been killed in Baltimore, destroyed by fire, it had to shake him up to realize that he was wrong. The knowledge of a fumble to destroy his confidence, for starters. Coupled with the understanding that Carboni didn't quit, regardless of the odds.

How many guys would make a comeback from the trauma he had suffered when they had the options of escape through suicide or drugs?

Damn few. Carboni couldn't think of one, in fact... unless it might be Bolan.

Fair enough.

From the beginning, he had sensed that they had much in common, like the two sides of the moon. One light, one dark. The soldier's problem was an out-of-date commitment to his fellow man—or woman—and that weakness was enough to get him killed. It was the edge Carboni needed, but it would not help him if he let his guard down and gave his adversary room to throw a sucker punch.

It was a treat to be alive, regardless, and he felt a sudden urge to celebrate.

The woman.

Perfect.

Vincent parked his Chevrolet inside the covered carport, killed the engine and remained behind the wheel for several moments, letting his anticipation build.

She would resist, of course. It was expected of her, and he would be disappointed if she didn't. Power was the prize, and proving it required a show of force. Surrender didn't mean a thing, except that you had chosen an unworthy adversary.

Vincent let himself in through the back, the same way he had brought Armato's gofer home a few short hours earlier. How much had changed within that time? Was he approaching the conclusion of his quest for vengeance? What, if anything, was waiting for him on the other side of Bolan's death?

It was a question he had never taken any time to ponder, what came *after*, and he wasted no time on the problem now. Tomorrow and the next day were beyond his grasp. Today he had Mack Bolan in his sights, and that was all Carboni cared about.

Except, just now, the woman.

He moved along a hallway to the master bedroom, where he left the Ingram and his automatic pistol on the dresser. There was no point in providing her with weapons, and Carboni knew that he could handle her just fine without the hardware. She was strong, but he was still a man, and he had picked up countless tricks for hand-to-hand encounters while he served the brotherhood.

It would be sweeter, knowing that she was—or had been—Bolan's woman. Something personal between them, serving almost as a prelude to the soldier's death. An overture, perhaps.

Carboni heard the shower as he stood outside her bedroom door, the key in hand. So much the better if he had an opportunity to take her by surprise. One more advantage for the home team in a game where odds were everything.

He closed the door behind him as he entered, pocketing the keys. The door couldn't be locked from this side, any more than it could be opened, but he wasn't concerned. If anything, it added just a touch of spice—the prospect of a possible escape to make his conquest real.

The bathroom door was closed, but he could hear the shower plainly now and he considered slipping in to join her. Picturing the woman wet and naked caused a stirring in Carboni's loins, but he restrained himself. The urge for dominance was one thing, but it would not do to have her scream and faint when she beheld his body, clothed in scars.

At times Carboni thought that the reaction he evoked from women was the worst of it. The pain had been a bitch, of course, but it was finally more or less behind him. The frank revulsion that he saw in women's eyes would last forever, and it galled him all the more because he had been decent looking in his day. False modesty aside, Carboni had been something of a ladies' man before the fire had robbed him of his looks. No Robert Redford maybe, but he kept himself in shape and did all right with women of the sort that turned him on. Before his run-in with the Executioner, it had been years since Vincent had to pay for sex.

These days, he had to pay *and* keep his fingers crossed, as some prostitutes drew the line at freaks. They didn't mind a threesome with the Bowery's finest, but many of them—most, in fact—were visibly repelled by Vincent's crinkled flesh, the shiny scalp beneath his so-expensive wig. The working girls who grudgingly agreed to take him on charged double, even triple, for a standard lay, and never mind the fancy stuff. Sometimes Carboni worked them over afterward to vent his anger and to show them that a freak has feelings, too.

The soldier's woman would be Vincent's first without a price tag since the fire. So much the better if she once belonged to Bolan. It was like poetic justice, when he thought about it. Chickens coming home to roost.

His slacks were suddenly too small, and Vincent smiled. All systems go. The night he nearly died, Carboni had been grateful that the flames had spared his feet. As time went on, he realized how very fortunate he was in other areas, as well. A few more minutes, if the rain hadn't arrived to wet him down, and Vincent might have died . . . or worse.

Oh, yes. Some things were worse than death. Carboni knew that from experience.

The Executioner would know it soon.

He heard the shower die and waited patiently for Val to dry herself. Carboni thought it would be time well spent. The shocked expression on her face, as she emerged, was everything he hoped for.

Vincent flashed his puckered grimace of a smile, his eyes feasting on the way her flannel nightgown clung to every luscious curve.

"You took your own sweet time," he said, "but it was worth it."

It took a moment, but she found her voice, relieved to find it steady as she spoke.

"Who are you?"

"I'm the guy who's gonna kill your boyfriend, with a little help from you."

"Don't hold your breath."

His hideous smile was mocking her. "Oh, you don't have to help, exactly. Being here's enough to start. It may be all I need."

"Where are we?"

"Does it matter? You're not going anywhere unless I say so. I'm the man, as far as you're concerned, from here on out."

She felt his eyes undressing her, and Val regretted standing underneath the icy spray that made her nipples hard. She would have given damn near anything just then for normal street clothes, underwear and all.

"I don't know who you think I am—"

"I *think* you're Valentina Gray," he told her, interrupting. "Or, perhaps I ought to say Querente. Pittsfield born and raised. I guess Wyoming's quite a switch, with all you've been through in your time."

"You have me at a disadvantage, Mr. . . . . ?"

"Yeah, I guess I do." He raised one hand—a claw, in fact, concealed within a special glove—and scratched behind a lumpish ear. "Just call me Vince. I'll call you Val. How's that?"

She glanced in the direction of the door. Would it be open? Could he lock it from the inside? And, if so, where would she find the key?

"I'm not sure what you mean about my 'boyfriend.' I'm a married woman."

"Yeah, I met your husband in the john." Her captor chuckled wetly. "And I think you know exactly what I mean. My old *compadres* at the headshed call him Mack the Bastard. He's the guy who fried my ass, or tried to. Trouble is, he didn't stick around to see it through."

"Too bad."

"For him . . . and you."

"Assuming you're correct, there's nothing I can do to help you."

"Oh, you're helping me right now, just being here. I left a message at your house to point him in the right direction, see?" He licked his withered lips. "I'll bet there's other ways that you could help me out, now that I think about it."

She braced herself to fight or flee, considering a back-step toward the bathroom, knowing she could never hold the door against determined opposition. He was tall—six feet or so, but the hat made estimates uncertain—and his slender build implied a wiry strength. Val wondered if the burns would slow him down, but she recalled no evidence of any handicap from their encounter at the house in Sheridan.

"What is it that you want?"

A stupid question. She could see it in his eyes, and on his person, but she was buying time. Perhaps she could take him by surprise, inflict sufficient damage to restrain him while she made it to the door . . .

"Right now," he said, "I want that nightgown off so we can get to know each other better."

"Go to hell."

"I've been there, babe. I came back, just for you."

She feinted to her left, in the direction of the door, and saw him shift to cut her off. Was it enough? No time for second thoughts as Val stepped forward, putting all her strength behind a well-aimed kick that ought to mash the family jewels if it connected squarely.

But he read her mind somehow and sidestepped, reaching out to trap her ankle at the moment when she meant to crush his scrotum, yanking sharply upward on her leg. The move threw Val off balance, and he took advantage of her posture, stepping forward, thrusting out a foot to cut her left leg from beneath her.

Val fell heavily, the impact emptying her lungs. A swarm of tiny flies swam in and out of focus as she twisted on the carpet, feeling her attacker as he dropped between her knees. She seemed to have no strength, but she resisted all the same, until his fist exploded in her face.

She felt the leather fingers of a glove inside the neckline of her flannel nightgown, ripping sharply downward, opening the garment like a robe in front. He pushed the useless flaps aside, exposing her, and Val was taken with a sudden chill that made her skin crawl. There was a momentary hesitation, then a whisper as he stripped the gloves away, before his fingers came back like creeping insects on her flesh.

"Not bad," he said. "Not bad at all."

She put her hopes, her final burst of strength, behind a lunge that brought her fingers toward his face, claws groping for his eyes. The stunning blow that rocked her backward seemed to come from nowhere, closing one of Valentina's eyes. Her skull smacked painfully against the floor, and in the hazy moment after impact, dazed, she offered up a silent prayer for darkness and oblivion.

Her only answer came from human lips, somewhere above her. Fearsome hands began to stroke her in a parody of tenderness.

"Don't fall asleep just yet," he chided her. "It's party time."

16

The telephone rang several times before Armato's house-man answered, sounding surly and suspicious.

"Yeah?"

"Put Nicky on."

"Who's this?"

"The name's Omega. I was out to see him yesterday."

"Oh, yeah. Hang on a second, will you?"

"Make it snappy, I don't have all day."

Mack Bolan waited while the guy went looking for Armato, picturing the would-be capo's face when he received the message. Nicky would be torn between relief and apprehension, wondering exactly what the "Black Ace" had discovered, anxious for the opportunity to try his hand against Chicago.

"This Omega?"

"Nicky?"

"Speaking."

"When's the last time that you checked your phones?"

"This morning. *Every* morning. They're as clean as they can be."

"You're sure?"

"I'd better be. I don't get out a lot these days."

"Okay. Which do you want up front, the good news or the bad?"

"Let's try the good. I need a change of pace."

"I've satisfied myself your recent troubles don't have anything to do with Bolan *or* Chicago."

"What the hell, you think it's my imagination? I've got people dying on the streets right now. We've taken half a dozen hits since you were here."

"I know that, Nicky."

"So? You want to fill me in, or what?"

"The bad news is, we've got a joker in the deck."

"I guess I don't quite follow you."

"You ever hear the name Carboni? *Vince* Carboni?"

"Yeah, it rings a bell. Just let me think a second. Wasn't he supposed to be some kind of hot mechanic? Yeah, he was an *Ace*, if I remember right."

"You hit in on the head. He *was*."

"I understand that something happened to him. He got hurt or something, and they had to dump him."

"Close, but no cigar. He got the hurt from Bolan, and he couldn't let it go. The board tried everything they could to calm him down, but he was like a wild man with a one-track mind. They had to let a contract on him in the end."

"So what?"

"The problem is, nobody ever tagged the crazy bastard. He's alive, and now he's got a hard-on for the brotherhood, just like he does for Bolan. Seems like he'll try anything to settle up old scores."

"He's got no beef with me," Armato said. "I never seen the guy before. What's this shit got to do with Denver?"

"Like I said, he lost it. This Carboni doesn't care who takes it in the shorts, as long as he gets even with the outfit. We've been tracking him around the country, here and there. He's pulled all kinds of crazy shit."

"You're telling me the Families combined can't tag one guy?"

"They couldn't pin a tail on Bolan, either."

"Shit. You saying this Carboni what's-his-name's as bad as Bolan?"

"Some say yes. Some say he's worse."

"How come I haven't heard about this sooner?"

"The big boys didn't get so big by airing their mistakes, okay? Imagine how you'd feel if you put out a hit on some guy, tried to whack him six or seven different times, and he kept coming back for more. Your people might lose confidence.''

''Well, Jesus Christ—''

''That isn't all of it.''

''Oh, no?''

''You keep a secret, Nicky?''

''Hey!''

''All right. The last six months or so, I'm hearing rumbles that Carboni might have made the tag on Bolan, but he's kept it to himself.''

''You think?''

''Suppose you took out Mack the Bastard, Nicky. What's the first thing you would do?''

''Put in a claim for the reward,'' Armato said without a trace of hesitation.

''Right. The same thing anybody else would do, if they were thinking right. But this Carboni's got a screw loose, maybe several. Just suppose he sees a way to keep the Executioner alive and use a dead guy's reputation to his own advantage.''

''Hitting on the brotherhood, you mean?''

''That's it. And while we're at it, let's go one step further. Say this crazy man is so far out of touch that he begins to think he *is* Mack Bolan.''

''What?''

''You've heard about these schizos, right? They don't know *who* the hell they are. Guy thinks he's Dracula or Julius Caesar, anybody. Hell, the loony bins are full of them.''

''Like *Psycho*, where the guy starts thinking he's his mother?''

''Right, like that.''

''I knew a guy once, in L.A., who used to act like he was Al Capone. I shit you not. He went around in these old-timey clothes, with spats and everything. Had some guy out in Hollywood make up a bunch of phony scars that he could plaster on his face. He used to get a lot of pussy with his act, don't ask me how. It was a laugh until he started showing up around the office with a fiddle case."

"What happened to him?"

"Oh, he died."

"Well, anyway, it's just a theory, but it seems to fit. The New York boys were talking to a shrink the other day, and this guy—some big name, a Jew downtown—says maybe Vince was so obsessed with Bolan that he really *loved* the guy instead of hating him."

"That's fucking weird."

"I'm telling you, the shrink's seen things like this before. He figured that Carboni spent so much time tracking Bolan down, he couldn't let it go, or he'd have nothing left. You follow? When the wiseguys tried to take him out, it made him *feel* like Bolan, with the brotherhood against him after all those years. A case like that, it's easy for a guy to snap."

"I don't like shrinks," Armato said. "They talk in circles and they take you nowhere."

"You ever talk to one?"

"Fuck, no!" The vehement reaction told him he had touched a nerve. "I know some guys that were referred from court, that's all. They told me how it was."

"I see."

Armato moved to change the subject. "Have you got a line on this Carboni guy?"

"Well, that's the kicker. Everything we've got so far points right to Denver."

"Tell me straight, now. Are you sure he isn't in with the Chicago crowd on this?"

"As far as I can tell, the guy's a solo act. I think your best bet would be to close ranks with Scimone and root the crazy bastard out before he buries both of you."

"If Patsy doesn't like the heat in Denver, he can go back home."

"Some guys I know might say the same about L.A."

"Check out your map. Who's Colorado closer to? Besides, we got here first."

"It's still an open territory. The Commission likes it that way, and I think it's safe to say they won't be happy with the guy who starts a shooting war."

"We've got the war already."

"Right, but with Carboni, not Chicago. Keep it that way, and the Families stand behind you. Try to make it something else, and you're out there on your own."

"I'm not exactly speaking to Scimone right now. I can't just call him up and ask him out for coffee."

"I'll be talking to him in a little while. With your permission, I'll arrange a meeting where the two of you can talk things over. Settle all your differences like gentlemen."

"You have the weight to set that up?"

"I have authority to settle the dispute, whichever way it goes."

Armato chewed on that one for a moment, finally deciding it was not a threat. "I don't go anywhere alone," he said at last. "Whatever kind of meeting you arrange, I can't be walking in there naked."

"Understood. You just sit tight now, and I'll set it up. When you and Patsy get things sorted out, we can get down to dealing with Carboni."

"Yeah, I guess." Armato didn't sound convinced.

"I'll be in touch."

Bolan severed the connection, smiling to himself. One down, and one to go. He lifted the receiver, dropped another coin and punched a second number up from memory.

"Hello?"

"Put Patsy on the line."

"Who says?"

"Just tell him it's Omega. He's been waiting for my call."

"Hang on."

He counted ninety seconds down before a gruff, familiar voice came on the line. "This who I think it is?"

"Depends. I've got a lone ace up my sleeve."

"Okay, what's shaking?"

"Can we talk on this line?"

"Yeah, it's clean. No problem."

"You're taking hits, I understand."

"Damn right. It's like a fucking nuthouse overnight. This Bolan has been wasting everything in sight."

"Not Bolan, Patsy."

"Huh?"

"You heard me."

"Yeah. I heard you yesterday, when you were in my house. You said—"

"I had it wrong, okay? It happens. I was thinking Bolan, just like you, but that's before I had a chance to check things out."

"I *knew* it! Nicky and his fucking L.A. crowd."

"It's not Armato, either."

"Oh? Who's left, the freaking Easter bunny?"

"You remember a mechanic by the name of Vince Carboni?"

"Yeah, I think I heard of him. So what?"

"Why don't you tell me what you heard."

"Is this the party line, or what? I don't have time for this."

"I'm asking you a simple question. Help me out, and you might help yourself."

"What the—Carboni was one of yours, as I recall."

"Go on."

"He had some kind of problem on a job. Got roasted, seems to me, but then he didn't croak. I understand he went a little haywire, and the board put out some paper on him."

"It's still out there."

"Yeah, I guess I heard that, too. Is there a point to this?"

"*He's* out there."

"We've established that. So what?"

"I think he's here in Denver."

"Bullshit. There's a price tag on the guy. I'd know if he was here."

"You didn't have a fix on Bolan, Patsy."

"That's a different story."

"Is it?"

"Everybody knows that Mack the Bastard has his own connections."

"*Had* connections. Past tense. We've got reason to believe he isn't with us anymore."

"You think somebody capped him and they're keeping it a secret? Boy, that's rich."

"Somebody with a reason, yeah."

"Like what? They've got a couple million reasons to be happy if they did the job. We'd have his head by now."

"Unless the shooter had a price tag on his own. Let's say he can't afford to take the credit, since he knows he won't collect the prize."

"Whatever you've been smoking, guy, you'd better tone it down."

"Let's say the shooter has a problem with the family *and* a use for Bolan's name."

"Carboni? Shit, you're dreaming. He's a refried coconut, for Christ's sake."

"He's been slick enough to burn down everyone the board's sent after him so far."

"You think *he* wasted Bolan?"

"It's a possibility."

"It sounds more like a fucking pipe dream. I suppose you think Carboni's shooting up my guys in Denver, too."

The Executioner let silence answer for him.

"Jesus Christ, you *do*. You think he's *here*."

"We *know* he's here. I couldn't tell you his address, but all the leads point straight to Denver."

"What about this other thing, the woman? Last night you were looking for this Bolan broad."

"Carboni has her." Bolan swallowed hard and said, "Or *had* her, anyway. The way I read it, he was hoping everyone would credit Bolan with the fireworks. By the time it all got sorted out, the place would be a fucking shambles and the Feds would be here, picking up the pieces."

"What about Armato?"

"What about him?"

"Well...I mean, he thinks he's got this territory sewn up for Los Angeles. He stands to gain if everybody else gets driven out of town."

"His boys are taking hits, the same as yours."

"My boys were taking hits *before*. You may be right about Carboni. I don't know, but I think Nicky had a setup working first, before the fruitcake ever got here."

"I'll be looking into that. Right now the board feels it's important for the two of you to patch things up and deal with the Carboni problem."

"Patch things up?" Scimone sounded clearly skeptical. "If you've got all this figured out, we don't have any reason to be fighting."

"Even so, I had a little talk with Nicky, and he seems to think you're gunning for him."

"Yeah? I can't imagine where he got that notion."

"It's the kind of thing we're trying to avoid. Right now the pigs and press think Bolan's kicking ass in Denver. Now, we all know Mack the Bastard's got a fan club, but the way things stand, a little fresh PR and you come out looking like the injured party. Nicky, too. You keep your cool—I don't care shit what anybody says—you come out looking like a gentleman. That's good for business in the long run."

"Yeah, okay. I guess I follow that."

"Now, you wade in with the troops, and that's a different story. Why's an honest businessman got all these guns and soldiers, anyway? Who's filling up the morgue when Bolan—or Carboni—does a fade and leaves you here to fight it out with Nicky on your own? That's *bad* for business, all around."

"You spoke to Nicky?"

"That I did."

"He goes along with this? I mean, about Carboni and the rest of it?"

"He had his doubts at first. I think we're seeing eye to eye right now."

"And what about Chicago?"

"He's suspicious, like I told you. I persuaded him to try a sit-down, but he can't pull off a meeting by himself."

Scimone was silent for a moment, thinking. "I don't like it."

"Hey, I understand. You've got your reservations, just like Nicky. If the two of you were bosom pals, we wouldn't need a meeting in the first place."

"Neutral ground? I can't be rolling into Lakewood, with the troops he's got in there."

"We didn't get that far. I'll tell you what. Why don't I pick a couple of spots and call you back. There must be somewhere both of you can feel at ease. And if there isn't . . . well, at least I tried."

"What's that supposed to mean?"

"I've got my orders, just like everybody else. The word is, don't come home until I've settled Denver."

"Settled? What the hell . . . ?"

"Hey, Patsy, we're both grown-ups here. You didn't think the board was gonna ask you nice and then forget it if a couple of lieutenants think they're bulletproof. This isn't the United Nations, where they talk a thing to death and then the small fry get to play their fucking games like no one gives a damn. The men in charge want peace and quiet. That's the bottom line."

"I don't like being threatened."

"No one does. Right now this three-ring circus threatens everything the outfit stands for. Something's got to give, and I mean soon."

"I settle up with Nicky now, and the Commission helps us tag Carboni?"

"That's the plan. I'm authorized to promise anything you need, across the board. He's playing with the big boys now. They mean to close his show."

"I get a vote on where we meet?"

"Just like I said."

"I don't like walking into this alone."

"Bring all the boys you need, but have them on their best behavior."

"My boys don't waste anyone else I tell them to."

"That's fair enough. I like a man who lets his people know who's boss."

"You'll be there?"

"If I can. The main thing is that you and Nicky iron things out."

"When this Carboni business is all taken care of, we may have to have another talk. I'm thinking of the split, for instance."

"One thing at a time, okay? The way you handle business in the next few days could have a lot to do with who comes out on top in Denver."

"Yeah? Well, Jeez, you should've told me that to start with."

"No one eats dessert before the meal."

"That's good." Scimone was chuckling to himself. "I like that."

"Yeah, I thought you might. Stay frosty, huh? I'll be in touch before you know it."

"I'll be here."

Bolan cradled the receiver, frowning as he backtracked to the Chrysler and his map of Denver to look for a piece of not-so-neutral ground.

17

He chose the railroad yards along the South Platte River after studying a Denver map and driving by to check the site himself. The setting was removed from residential streets and major business areas, providing ample combat stretch in case the play developed as he hoped. At night there would be few employees in the yard, and idle cars would offer adequate concealment in the early stages of his plan.

In short the killing ground was perfect—or, as close to perfect as the Executioner would find within the time allowed.

He called Armato first and won the L.A. mobster's grudging acquiescence to a meet on neutral ground at nine o'clock. It was decided that an honor guard of three crew wagons was acceptable, and Bolan thereby fixed the California team at roughly twenty guns.

So far, so good.

Scimone had tried to move the rendezvous, protesting that the drive was nearly twice as far from his house to the railroad yards as from Armato's. Bolan countered with a thinly veiled insinuation that "the boys upstairs" would not be overly amused by petty arguments at that stage of the game, and Patsy canceled his objections after Bolan granted leave for him to bring an extra car along.

That made it thirty guns to L.A.'s twenty, give or take, but Bolan was not laying odds on either side. His main concern was with a solitary gunner lurking somewhere on the sidelines, presently beyond his reach.

A third call tipped Brognola to the time and place of Armageddon, leaving him to make arrangements on his own for any mop-up he desired. Whatever happened, he would do his best to stall the cavalry by ten or fifteen minutes, giving Bolan ample time to spot his target and engage.

Provided that Carboni took the bait.

It was a problem, granted, but the Executioner was forced to base his strategy on qualified assumptions. He assumed, for instance, that Carboni had a line on Nicky or Scimone—or both—to keep him briefed on current movements in the Family. It didn't matter, for the soldier's purposes, if Vince was operating through informers, bugs or ESP, as long as he was somehow tipped about the evening's meet.

Once he had tumbled to the move in progress, it would be a golden opportunity for Bolan's nemesis to strike another blow against his chosen enemies. And having once revealed himself...

The rest of it got hairy, trusting luck as much as skill, but Bolan had no choice. If he could spot Carboni, he would give the rogue Ace room to run, and this time he would not be shaken off the track. If Vincent's mind was running true to form—and Val was still alive—the one-time mafioso just might lead him home.

But if not, the Executioner was bent on making this Carboni's final night on earth, no matter how the game played out. If he could rescue Val, so much the better, but Carboni's ticket would be canceled either way.

Unless his target missed the showdown.

Bolan closed his mind to negative transmissions, concentrating on the positive. He *would* destroy Carboni and complete the work begun in Baltimore so long ago. Val *would* return, intact, to Jack and Johnny.

Concentrating on his hardware, piece by piece, he waited for the night to fall.

"YOU HEARD ME RIGHT," Brognola snapped into the telephone. "I want the Bureau SWAT teams from Kansas City *and* Los Angeles. They should be here and suited up by eight o'clock, my time.''

He listened briefly to objections from the other end, his craggy features sculpted in a frown. ''I honestly don't give a shit if K.C. *is* committed to a practice run-through for the governor. That's right. If L.A. has a problem while I'm borrowing her troops, the San Francisco team can cover. Right. Okay. You have your orders, then. Get on it.''

Dropping the receiver in its cradle, he expelled a weary sigh and swiveled in his chair to glance at Leo Turrin. ''Pencil pushers. Jesus Christ, you'd think I asked for nukes or something, with the static I've been getting.''

''Are they coming?''

''Bet your ass,'' Brognola said. ''I may not have a job this time next week, but we'll have troops tonight.''

''That's what, a dozen men?''

''Fourteen.'' Brognola frowned again. ''It isn't much. I'd better check and see if anybody in the Denver office has been trained for special weapons.''

''Done,'' said Leo. ''They've got two men standing by at your disposal.''

''Great. With you and me, that means we'll only be outnumbered two or three to one.''

''Sounds like the good old days.''

''The old days weren't so good, my friend. We're in a world of hurt if this goes wrong, and even money says we're blowing smoke.''

''You think Carboni may not show?''

''I don't know what to think. The boys at Quantico assure me he's a fruitcake. Hell, for all I know he's halfway to the coast by now and chasing men from Mars.''

''But Striker doesn't think so.''

''No.''

''And I don't, either.''

''The eternal optimist.''

''Carboni may be out there in the twilight zone,'' said Leo, ''but he has a solid fix on Striker in his mind. I don't believe he went through all this pain and planning just to blow it off and walk away before he does his job.''

"I hope you're right."

"We're not exactly swamped with options."

"No."

Brognola thought about it. Sixteen members of the Bureau SWAT team, plus himself and Turrin. Call it eighteen guns against an estimated fifty hardmen—more, if Nicky and Scimone decided to ignore the ground rules for the meeting.

It was like old days, right. The *bad* old days.

"There's always Striker," Leo told him, tuning in Brognola's wavelength from across the room.

"No good. He's on Carboni if the bastard shows."

"Don't sell him short."

And Turrin had a point, of course. Once Bolan took a job, he saw it through. The guy had never failed Brognola yet.

But every set was different, damn it. Any play could blow up in your face, and Bolan was no more immortal than the next man.

Granted, he had played against the odds so long and so successfully that sometimes Hal was prone to think of him as Mr. Miracle, the warrior who could never fail. A major part of that was wishful thinking, friendship leaking through to taint Brognola's judgment, but the rest of it was based on Bolan's knack for pulling off the moves that others thought of as impossible.

The old days.

Hal was feeling older all the time, and it occurred to him that neither one of them had slept since early yesterday.

"You tired?"

"Not really. You?"

Brognola shook his head. How long since Bolan had the time to close his eyes and sleep? Would he find any peace in dreams, or were they merely a continuation of his everlasting war?

"You said the Denver office has some men on standby?"

"Two."

"We might as well go introduce ourselves," Brognola said. "We'll have to draw some extra hardware anyway."

He checked his watch as they were leaving the motel room. Seven hours left till show time, and he didn't even want to think about what happened afterward.

Ten minutes, he had promised Bolan. Fifteen, tops. It was a lifetime for the soldiers on the firing line.

For some, Brognola thought, it would be all the time they had.

"THREE CARS," Armato said. "How many soldiers can we manage, Joey?"

His lieutenant was a rock named Joe Lolordo, fifteen kills that Nicky knew about for sure. The guy had seen it all. His face was carved in stone.

"You pack 'em in and use the jump seats, I can give you eight guys in a car. That's twenty-four, less one seat for yourself."

"Okay, then. Squeeze them all you have to. Everybody's packing heavy, and I mean the drivers, too."

"No problem," Joey said, but he was frowning to himself.

"What is it?"

"Nothing, Mr. A. It ain't my place."

"Since when? Come on, already. What's the problem?"

"Well . . . I thought this was supposed to be some kind of treaty talk."

"That *is* what it's supposed to be," Armato said. "The trouble is, I don't know this Omega from the next guy on the street, and I don't trust Scimone as far as I can throw this house."

"You think Omega's scamming?"

"It's possible," Armato said. "I made some calls last night, out west and other places. No one will admit they ever heard of him, except a friend of mine in Philly thought that he was dead."

Lolordo shrugged. "It's hard to pin these Aces down," he said, "the way they move around so much. I heard of one guy, used to have a different name for every town he worked in. These days..."

He left it hanging, but Armato got the point. Too many damn loose ends, and there was no way he could ever check them out unless he started calling up Commission members on his own.

Fat chance.

Omega was a nagging question mark, just like his tale about Carboni. Sure, the story of the Ace gone bad had been around, and Nicky was familiar with the basic details, but the rest of it—the crap about a toasted psycho with a Bolan complex—was enough to make him laugh out loud.

Except that guys were getting killed in Denver, right and left, by Bolan or a damn persuasive copycat. And if it was Carboni... then what?

"Did that put Patsy and Chicago in the clear, without a second thought? Who said that Vince Carboni had it in for every member of the brotherhood across the board?"

Omega said so, right.

But what if he was wrong or lying through his teeth? Suppose Omega *was* Carboni, maybe with a face-lift, dusting off his old black ace to make some mischief in the ranks. Suppose he still had friends around the Windy City, with a sanctuary all lined up in Denver once he helped them make their move.

Armato wondered if his life-style had begun to make him paranoid, and he decided that it didn't matter one way or the other. He had never seen a wiseguy killed by too much caution, but the list of careless dead went on and on. The moment you began to let yourself relax, becoming over-confident, there was a smart-ass waiting in the wings to knock you off and take your place.

Some life.

But it was Nicky's, and he would not honestly have traded it for anybody else's he could think of. Power was the key, and he had done all right in that department, yes indeed.

Okay, he didn't have a Family of his own so far, but Denver was a start, and he could flex more muscle in his own backyard than many of the nation's so-called leaders ever could.

Suppose the President got tired of someone bitching at him all the time and taking shots behind his back. What could he do? The poor schmuck had to go through channels like a fucking civil servant, with the Congress breathing down his neck along the way. Forget about it if he tried to make somebody disappear. The press would have his balls for breakfast, and by suppertime he would be history.

It made Armato feel a little better when he put things in perspective, but he still had problems with the meet.

"You checked the switchyard out?" he asked Lolordo.

Joey nodded. "I sent two boys over, and they had a look around. It seems okay. I'd like to send a couple of our guys in early, just in case."

"You do that, Joey. Stash them somewhere so they don't get spotted by the railroad dicks, but they can be there if we need them. Later, if it all pans out, Scimone don't have to know that they were ever there."

"And if it don't pan out—"

"We got him by the balls," Armato said, surprised to find the smile came easily. "He can't sneak anybody past us, and we've got a couple extra soldiers in a pinch."

"I'll handle it," Lolordo said.

Armato rose to pour himself a drink. He didn't offer one to Joey, knowing that his second-in-command would never touch a drop on duty. Suddenly he felt like celebrating.

If Scimone was on the up-and-up, their truce would give Armato time to reinforce his Denver stronghold, mobbing up against a future push by the Chicago hardforce. On the other hand, if Patsy tried to pull a fast one, L.A.'s baddest would be set to rock and roll.

Armato checked his Rolex. Six more hours, give or take.

He found that he could hardly wait.

TEN MILES AWAY on Windsor Lake, Pasquale Scimone was also huddled with his number two, a heavy hitter by the name of Rocco Fanelli. In Chicago, Rocco had the reputation of being a one-man gang, implacable and merciless in combat. Sending Rocco on to Denver with Scimone had been a gesture on the part of Don Pagano, telling anyone who cared to listen that the peasants shouldn't fuck around with his Chicago troops.

And now he had to wade through all this crap with Nicky, Mack the Bastard and Carboni. It was bad enough when they were squaring off for a potential war against Los Angeles without a nod from the Commission. Bolan made the whole thing ten times worse, and now...well, Patsy couldn't make his mind up *what* the hell was going on.

"You ever meet this Vince Carboni, Rocco?"

"Nah. I heard about him, though."

"He any good?"

An easy shrug. "He was an Ace."

That said it all or should have, but the past tense was a clinker. If the stories Patsy heard were true, Carboni had been damn near fried back East somewhere. You don't bounce back so easy from a thing like that, and something in his mind had snapped along the way. A crazy man was dangerous, but he had weak points, too. For starters he would have to do without his old connections in the brotherhood, and that meant he was on his own.

"Or was he?"

"You know if he was tight with anybody special?"

"Who? Carboni?"

"No, the fucking Easter bunny, Rocco. Who'd you think?"

The heavy hitter never turned a hair. He knew which side his bread was buttered on.

"Them Aces ain't supposed to play no favorites," he said. "It's democratic, like. They used to work for the Commission, under Pat and Mike, but these days..."

"Yeah?"

Another shrug, disinterested.

"You hear all kinds of stories," Fanelli said. "Some guys'll tell you that the Aces ain't around no more. I figure there's a few of them, but they're reserved for special numbers, like."

"No local tie-ins?"

"Used to have their headshed in New York. I never heard of anybody special being tied up with L.A."

"That's what I thought."

But Patsy wasn't betting anybody's life—and least of all his own—on recollections of the way things used to be. The world had turned a time or two since Pat and Mike were running things for the Commission's hard arm, and the Aces that survived, if any, were becoming an endangered species. There was nothing to prevent a savvy operator from acquiring special friends, and if those friends were in Los Angeles...

"Carboni lost his marbles, huh?"

"That's what they say."

"Did anybody send him to a shrink?"

That brought a smile from Rocco. "Nah," he said. "They tried to clip him, but he don't clip easy."

"What's his price?"

"Two hundred thou, the last I heard. Nobody's seen him in a while."

"You met this guy Omega. What's your reading?"

Fanelli thought about it for a moment, chewing on his lower lip. "He's got the look. A guy like that, the people that he's whacked, you see 'em in his eyes."

"I wish to hell we knew who he was working for."

"One guy, he can't do much."

"That's what they used to say about this Bolan."

"Piece of cake," the heavy hitter said. "We're going in with more than thirty people."

"Just make sure you keep them on their toes."

"No sweat."

"I mean, if this is straight, we play it straight for now. I don't want any flash unless Armato tries to pull a number."

"If he does, you want that I should whack Omega?"

Patsy thought about it for a moment, weighing odds and angles.

"Hold that thought," he said.

BY SUNDOWN Bolan had his place picked out among the boxcars. He had waited for the day shift to depart, the smaller night shift clocking in, and he had watched them from a distance as they went about their duties. When he had their schedules and routines in mind, he made his move.

After one trip to transfer hardware from the Chrysler, parked outside the railroad yard, Bolan settled in a stock car. It was one of several on a siding near the point where two uneasy warlords were supposed to meet in approximately three hours' time. He stashed his basic weapons in a corner, out of sight, and took one satchel with him as he left the car.

The blacksuit and his camo war paint helped him use the shadows as he crept across the yard, alert to any workers deviating from their rounds. His first stop was a flatcar on another siding, where he slithered underneath and lay between the rails, the heavy satchel on his chest.

He placed the charge of C-4 plastique near the middle of the car for maximum effect and molded it to give the blast more lift than spread. The detonator he implanted in the mass of lethal putty would acknowledge signals from a mile away, and Bolan meant to shave that distance to an easy fifty yards.

When he was finished with the flatcar, Bolan doubled back along the line and chose a boxcar marked with rust spots and graffiti. Once inside the car, he packed two smaller charges, fore and aft, against the nearest wall. On detonation they would open up the boxcar like a beer can with a cherry bomb inside, and all that rusty steel would serve as shrapnel. When his work was done, he had himself a giant claymore set on wheels.

The rest was waiting in his stock car with the M-16 and Uzi by his side. Fatigue attempted to distract him, but he kept his mind alert and focused on the odds against him, concentrating on the different ways his plan could still go wrong.

If either Nicky or Scimone decided not to play and scrubbed the meeting. If Carboni failed to show, or satisfied himself with watching from the sidelines while the troopers from Chicago and L.A. went up in flames.

Too many *ifs* for Bolan to consider each of them in turn.

The game was set and ready to begin.

He settled back and waited for the other players to arrive.

18

Carboni had Armato's house staked out when things began to happen shortly after eight o'clock. He had been running out of targets lately, and decided that it wouldn't hurt to watch the big boys for a while. At any time one of them would make a break or send some runners out for bagels—anything at all. He might as easily have picked Scimone, but Nicky's place was on a narrow side street and provided more concealment.

Besides, Carboni needed rest.

The woman had surprised him with her strength, but he had broken her the way he broke all opposition. There was really nothing to it if you knew the moves. He hoped that there would be sufficient time for one more private bout before he wrapped things up in Denver, but he knew the action couldn't last much longer.

Bolan was a classic blitzkrieg artist, hit and run, guerrilla style. He never hung around one place too long, aware that he was vulnerable standing still. The first time out, in Pittsfield, he had spent a month around the old home neighborhood, and it had nearly killed him.

But a crafty soldier always learned from his mistakes.

If something was about to break in Denver, it had to come within the next two days, perhaps that very night. He would not put it past the Executioner to try a raid on Nicky or Scimone at home, and since he couldn't cover both of them at once, he had to make a choice. The scanner on the seat beside him would alert Carboni if Scimone had any uninvited company.

In fact Carboni was prepared for damn near anything, except the convoy. Three crew wagons rolling through the gates and headed east on Jewell, with gunners packed in like sardines. He couldn't tell if Nicky was among them, but it didn't matter. That much armor on the move meant action, and Carboni wanted it.

He gave the tanks a lead and fell in place behind them, running in their shadow, switching off his lights from time to time to keep the tail man guessing. They ran arrow-straight on Jewell until they picked up Federal, turning north.

He scratched Scimone's home base as a potential target, sticking with the caravan as it continued north. They took their time, as if arriving at their destination was the last thing on their minds. Carboni knew you didn't roll this kind of muscle if you didn't mean it, but the general direction of their travel told him nothing.

He was with them when they breezed past Barnum Park and picked up Highway 6, due east. An easy quarter-mile, and then he tracked them through the interchange, a looping cloverleaf that fed them onto Highway 25 northbound.

Strange. There were no major targets in this direction, at least not that Carboni was aware of. Could it be that Nicky was abandoning his post and striking off for somewhere safe outside the city? Should he disengage before they led him out of town and made him miss whatever might be happening in town?

Carboni got his answer as the lead car caught an exit ramp to Larimer, the others following. He trailed them like a jackal following a pride of lions, his curiosity revived now that they seemed to have a destination fixed in mind.

From Larimer the limos wound through narrow side streets, with Vincent hanging farther back until they reached the railroad yards. The chain-link gate they chose had been secured with chains, but as Carboni watched, a soldier from the lead car solved that problem with a pair of heavy bolt-cutters, rolling the gate aside as sweet as you please. The limos passed inside and disappeared from view.

Now what the hell?

He knew that Nicky's troops had not come down to greet a train—that much was obvious from their approach. A meeting, then, but why the railyards?

In a flash he had the answer, and his pulse was hammering. Armato needed neutral ground because he had arranged a meeting with Scimone. No matter how he turned the thing around and looked at it from different angles, nothing else made sense.

Armato and Scimone, together. Could the Executioner be far behind?

Carboni found himself a place to park his Chevrolet and lingered long enough to choose a weapon from the trunk. He liked the Steyer AUG because it was a handy compact piece—a rifle with the overall dimensions of a submachine gun. Carrying the weapon openly, with extra magazines protruding from his pockets, Vince Carboni crossed the street and slipped inside the darkened railyard.

This time, if the Executioner appeared, it would be Vincent's turn to pick the moment. And if Bolan didn't make the party, there was still tomorrow. After he had raised some hell between Chicago and L.A.

It was the least that he could do, considering how much the brotherhood had done for him. Carboni owed them something special, and he was about to pay this debt, with interest due.

BOLAN WAS IN PLACE and waiting when the limos started to arrive. Three cars at first, and that would be Armato, several minutes early to check out the site. Observing their arrival from his place inside the nearby stock car, Bolan wondered which side had dispatched the men who lay behind him in the dark.

All things considered, it was a decent plan, and if Bolan had not taken up his post at sundown it might have worked. As it was, he made the infiltrators quickly, watched them huddle in the shadow of a truck barn, choosing lookout points before they split. He was in motion and closing in by the time his first selected target settled into a caboose some twenty yards away.

The doors had been removed, presumably for maintenance, and Bolan had no trouble slipping in behind the gunner, Ka-Bar fighting knife in hand. The guy's attention was completely focused on the yard, believing that he had it knocked by showing up an hour ahead of time. He never heard death coming for him, creeping up behind.

It was a textbook move, the left hand clamped across his mouth and nose as Bolan twisted, cutting off his wind. The eight-inch blade slid home between his ribs, and Bolan held him as he shuddered through the final microseconds of his life.

When it was over, Bolan took the gunner's weapon, hoisted deadweight in a fireman's carry and retraced his steps in the direction of the stock car. Time was running out, and he would have to take the second gunner out before the guests of honor started to arrive.

His man was crouching in a boxcar with open doors on both sides as the Executioner approached. As with his late companion, he was concentrating on the meeting ground, prepared to use the Ingram submachine gun that he carried if a member of the opposition turned up early or the meet went sour.

He never got the chance.

From where he stood in shadow, Bolan knew he couldn't risk the knife a second time. It would have been impossible for him to board the car and close to killing range before his adversary brought the Ingram into play, and even if the gunner failed to score a hit, the noise would ruin everything.

He drew the silent 93-R from its armpit sheath and braced it in a classic target stance, his sight fixed on a point behind one ear. A gentle squeeze, and Bolan saw the lookout melt away, his weapon sliding to the boxcar's floor. Another heavy-laden trek to Bolan's hiding place, and he was clear.

Then the limos came.

He watched Armato's three cars pull up in a line, the middle vehicle directly opposite the tank car he had primed with C-4 plastique. It was perfect. Bolan took the two small detonators from his belt, armed both of them and set them on the floor before himself. Their tiny red lights glowed in the darkness of the car.

Ten minutes passed, and Nicky's troops were getting restless when another minicaravan arrived. Scimone was right on time, with four cars full of muscle to protect him. Bolan watched in satisfaction as the new arrivals drew up, two abreast, the tail cars well within the striking range of Bolan's loaded boxcar. Thirty feet of open ground lay in between the hostile forces as they studied one another, with the Executioner directly opposite.

There was no sign of Vince Carboni yet. No way of telling if the lure had been successful.

Bolan chose the Uzi, flicked its safety off and started counting down.

"HE BROUGHT a fucking army with him," Nicky snapped. "What is this shit?"

"No sweat," said Joe Lolordo, riding in the limo's shotgun seat. "You count our early birds, and we can't be down by more than six or seven guys."

"I still don't like it, Joey. Make damn sure that everybody's on their toes. If one of those Chicago bastards makes a move, I want him roasted on the spot. Don't wait for me."

"You got it, boss."

Lolordo muttered orders to the walkie-talkie in his hand, and gunners started to unload on either side of Nick Armato. On the other side of no-man's-land, he saw the soldiers from Chicago doing likewise, fanning out around their cars. Armato didn't like the setup, but he had already come this far, and backing out without a face-to-face would be a frank admission of defeat.

The pavement had a gritty feel beneath his shoes. Armato slipped the single button on his tailored jacket, granting instant access to the .45 inside his waistband. Picking out

Scimone in the opposing crowd, he wondered where his early birds had placed themselves. If nothing else, he hoped they had the sense to scope on Patsy and to take him out at once if anything went wrong.

"Stay frosty," he commanded, speaking to his strong right arm.

"We've got it covered," Joey told him, smiling.

But Nicky still had doubts about the whole damn thing, and they weren't diminished by the absence of Omega from the scene. He should have been there, since he had been the one to set the meeting in the first place.

Getting paranoid, he thought. No time to fall apart when he was looking at Chicago's baddest, eye to eye. The situation called for nerves of steel and balls of solid brass.

Armato wondered if he had not bitten off a little more than he could chew, and then he pushed the thought away before it had a chance to undermine his confidence.

"Okay," he said to no one in particular, "let's get it done."

"THOSE BOYS are packing heavy," Rocco Fanelli told Scimone.

Chicago's pointman in the Rockies made a sour face and answered, "So are we."

It made him nervous, all the same, to stand this close and feel so many gunners itching for a chance to open fire. If anybody sneezed or tried to scratch his balls, the whole damn thing could come apart. And where the hell was this Omega, anyway.

Scimone pushed past his number two and raised his voice to hail Armato. "Nicky, you've got company."

"You're not exactly by yourself," Armato countered.

"What the hell, the way things have been going lately, everybody's got the right to be a little nervous."

"Maybe."

Patsy didn't like the smug tone. "We here to talk a deal or what?"

"Depends. Somebody owes me for the damage to my property and all the help I lost."

"I haven't raised a hand against your men so far. Besides, you're not the only one's been taking hits the past few days."

Armato chewed on that one for a moment, looking thoughtful. "You been talking to Omega?"

"We had words. I thought he was supposed to be here."

"Maybe he's got other things to do. You think we need a referee?"

"I'll tell you what I think. When I see open territory, I assume it's anybody's game. I don't expect to have my people whacked because they try to earn a living."

"Times are changing, Patsy. Maybe calling Denver open territory wasn't such a hot idea."

"It's funny you should say that. I've been thinking pretty much the same."

"It would appear we have a problem, then."

"I'd say that's right."

"You ever hear about first come, first served?"

"I heard a different one. The strong survive."

"You wouldn't have a little something up your sleeve, now, would you Patsy? Like an Ace, for instance?"

The passing reference to Carboni made Scimone glance furtively toward the surrounding shadows.

"I've been hearing stories. If you think he's one of mine, you got it wrong."

"It's hard to swallow, one man doing it for spite."

"You got a better reason?"

"Maybe he's on call."

Scimone could feel the angry color rising in his cheeks. "If I had something on my mind, I wouldn't use a burn-out psycho for the pointman."

"For a burn-out, he's been doing pretty good so far."

"And I suppose the guy's been hitting me for fun? Does that make any sense to you?"

Armato hesitated for a moment, knowing that it made no sense at all.

"You want to know what I think?" he replied at last. "Here goes."

But Patsy never heard his opposition's words of wisdom. They were lost forever, blown away and scattered as the world exploded in his face.

"ALL SET?"

Brognola moved along the line of men in caps and jumpsuits marked with the initials of the FBI. They carried M-16s and riot guns, a couple of them packing sniper rifles fitted out with scopes for sighting in the dark. Their nylon harnesses were hung with side arms, ammunition pouches, stun grenades and other items of equipment.

"Ready," said the chief of Kansas City's team.

"Let's do it," added the honcho from L.A.

"Before we roll," Brognola said, "remember that you'll be outnumbered roughly three to one. These guys don't have your training, but they've been around, and every one of them has made his bones. They won't care shit about a badge or warrant."

One of Denver's agents cleared his throat. "What *is* the charge we're moving on?"

"Officially we want Armato and Scimone for questioning on racketeering counts. I've got the paperwork on those two, plus a couple dozen John Doe warrants charging violation of the firearms act. If things get hot tonight, we'll have new charges down the line. More questions?"

There were none, and Hal retrieved his riot shotgun from a table by the door as they were filing out to take their places in the waiting vans. Beside him, Leo Turrin seemed at home in cap and jumpsuit, handling an M-16.

"Be careful, Leo. You're enjoying this."

"Not yet." The grin gave way at once to a more thoughtful attitude. "You think he'll pull it off?"

"The meet? No problem. Pinning down Carboni may be something else."

"No problem with the locals?"

"It was touch and go," Brognola said, remembering the Denver chief's suspicious glare. "I had to sign a chit accepting full responsibility for anything that happens if it blows."

"That's cute."

"No choice. If Striker puts it on the line, the least that I can do is bet the pension."

"Still no line on Val?"

"There won't be till he has Carboni in the bag."

"*Damn*, I wish that there was something we could do. I can't forget the time when Angelina—"

"Yeah," Brognola cut him off. "Me, too."

The Executioner had helped them both at one time or another when the lives of loved ones had been riding on the line. It galled him now that he was relegated to the role of batting cleanup while his closest friend outside of wedlock faced the heavy hitters on his own. It wasn't fair, but that was life—and death—in Bolan's world.

He followed Turrin to the vans, peeled off toward number one while Leo took the second. "Don't get lost," he chided, straining for a note of levity.

"Fat chance."

He settled in the shotgun seat and nodded to the driver. "Nice and slow," he said. "We've still got twenty minutes and we can't afford to show up early."

"Ruins the surprise, I guess?"

"You might say that."

Brognola felt the van begin to move, but he couldn't have named the streets they crossed or those they traveled, headed for the killing ground. His mind was there already, trying to imagine what it took to face those kinds of odds alone, to gamble everything you cared about on one roll of the dice.

And knowing what it took, before he really had to think about it.

At the bottom line, it took a man like Bolan, and there weren't enough of them to go around.

Not nearly enough.

Brognola kept his fingers crossed and prayed he would not lose the only one he had.

"YOU WANT TO KNOW what I think?" Nick Armato snarled across the distance that separated him from the Chicago troops. "Here goes."

The Executioner had heard enough. He keyed the detonator on his right and rode the shock wave as the flatcar buckled, folding almost double, rising on a tongue of flame. He saw a number of Armato's gunners flattened by the blast, their limos rocking from the force of the concussion.

Number two was keyed a heartbeat later, C-4 plastique charges ripping through the boxcar, chunks of white-hot shrapnel peppering Chicago's ranks like grapeshot. Two or three of Patsy's men were damn near vaporized on impact, others going down with wounds that ranged from superficial to severe. The armor plating on Scimone's crew wagons also took a beating, jagged rents appearing in the bodywork.

Before the shaken mobsters could recover, Bolan poked his Uzi through the stock car's slats and fired a burst from left to right, his gunfire adding to the general din of cries and echoes. No one saw precisely where the hostile fire was coming from, and at the moment no one seemed to care. It was enough to know that *someone* had begun the action, and a score of guns erupted up and down the tattered firing line.

He lifted off the trigger, searching for Armato and Scimone in the confusion as their soldiers started trading shotgun blasts and burst of automatic fire. The honchos were survivors, and he saw that both of them had gone to ground immediately, each man looking out for number one.

The buttons, meanwhile, looked for cover near the limousines or scattered toward the nearest railroad cars, each side intent on circling behind their enemies to gain a slim advantage in the crunch. They didn't have much time, he knew, before employees dropped a dime and summoned the police.

He wondered if Brognola had been able to arrange for a delay. It had to go against the grain for local officers to stand aside and leave the game to Uncle Sam. They might not play along, and if they didn't, Bolan's plan had even less chance of success.

The Executioner had never killed a cop and didn't plan to. At the first sight of a black-and-white, he would be forced to disengage. Carboni had a few more moments to reveal himself, if he was here at all. Beyond that time...

A member of the L.A. team was running straight for Bolan's stock car, counting on its bulk to shelter him while he continued sniping at the enemy. He changed his mind too late, and Bolan's Uzi stuttered from between the slats, a line of parabellum crushers ripping him from crotch to throat and blowing him away.

A shotgun blast punched through the wooden siding overhead, and Bolan knew he had been spotted by the enemy. So much for lying low and playing both ends off against the middle. Nicky's gunners would suppose that he was playing for Chicago now. As for Scimone...

No time for speculation, as an automatic rifle started punching holes around him. Bolan answered with a final Uzi burst, retrieved his M-16 and hit the other door at speed. It was a four-foot drop, and Bolan landed in a crouch, immediately moving out to find another vantage point from which to carry on the fight.

Unwillingly he forced the image of Carboni from his mind and concentrated on survival. He would be no good to Val—to anyone—if he was dead, and carelessness could definitely get him killed. A soldier with his mind on other things had no damn business on the firing line.

The Executioner let instinct be his guide. The scent of carnage was his lure.

It smelled like home.

19

Bolan hit the ground running as bullets and buckshot rattled the slats in the stock car behind him. He passed a flat car, ducking low to rob the marksmen of a silhouette, and pulled up short behind another boxcar, breathing heavily.

How many button men had spotted him? Considering the chaos on the field, he estimated that it would have been no more than three or four on either side, and none of them would know which side the phantom gunner was supporting. Out of sight beyond the boxcar, guns were hammering a steady beat. Despite the close-range blasts, both sides apparently had men and arms enough to keep the battle going at a fever pitch.

He looped the Uzi's strap across one shoulder, carrying the M-16 and M-203 launcher as he edged around a corner of the boxcar. Twenty yards in front of him, the warring sides were giving one another hell with everything they had, some soldiers huddled near the limousines while others sniped from railroad cars where they had taken cover. Bolan estimated that Scimone still had about two dozen gunmen able to defend themselves against perhaps fourteen or fifteen for Armato. He would have to shave the odds a bit before Brognola and the cavalry arrived.

He fed the launcher with a high-explosive round and let it fly downrange, impacting on the lead car in Armato's caravan. The limo bucked and reared, flames billowing beneath it, doors blown open, armored windows shattered by the blast. A human comet streaked across the battlefield, arms beating at the hungry flames until a burst of automatic gunfire dropped him in his tracks.

Nobody seemed to know where the explosive charge had come from, so he held his ground and loaded up another, swiveling to find a target on Scimone's side of the killing ground. A trigger stroke, and Bolan watched another car disintegrate, its trunk lid soaring skyward on a spout of flaming gasoline from the erupting fuel tank. Several men were flattened by the blast, and Bolan raked them with a long burst from the M-16 as they began to rise again.

The muzzle-flashes marked him, and a couple of Armato's gunners spotted him at once. They hesitated, noting the direction of his fire, perhaps believing he was one of the advance men sent ahead to lay an ambush, and he solved the riddle for them with a blazing figure-8 that blew them both away.

Behind the last of the surviving L.A. tanks, another button saw it happen, and he opened fire on Bolan with a submachine gun, bullets rattling off the boxcar, gouging asphalt at his feet. Instead of dueling with the gunner, Bolan left him to it, jogging down the line of cars until he had placed roughly forty yards between the battle and himself.

It was a chance that he would have to take. He needed new perspective on the action, and the only way to flush Carboni out—assuming he was even here—would be for Bolan to reveal himself. Without a solid target, Vince might be content to hang back in the shadows, cheating Bolan of another chance to close his show.

He made his break across the open ground and sets of rails, the battle raging on his right. How long before Brognola and the rest arrived? He had a nagging sense that he was running out of time.

Secure once more, he worked his way along the line of railroad cars in the direction of the firing. Two cars short of the demolished flatcar, Bolan nearly stumbled on a gunner from Armato's team crouched down behind a flatcar, seeking shelter from the storm. The slacker came alive at sight of Bolan, and the warrior clipped him with a backstroke from his rifle butt, the impact staggering his adversary. In a blur of motion, Bolan followed through, a sharp knee to the groin, another to the face and one sharp blow across the throat—now suddenly exposed—to finish it.

It would have been a simple thing to shoot the man, but he was trying for position now and didn't care to telegraph his move. The warring mafiosi might have missed it, anyway, but you could never tell.

He passed the twisted, mangled wreckage of the flatcar, feeling heat that radiated from the blackened steel. A few more yards, and he would be in the position he desired. From there—another stock car, as it happened—Bolan would again be able to bring both sides under fire if he desired.

He took the time to check his watch. Six minutes in and counting. That meant Hal was on the way, and once the uniforms arrived, his chances of a contact with Carboni would be nil.

God *damn* it! Was Carboni there or not?

He settled in between the stock car and its neighbor, snapping a fresh magazine into the assault rifle as he scanned the field for targets. They were numerous enough, but Bolan wanted something special. He was not content just now to spray the ranks at random. Bolan wanted something special, something worth his time.

He found it in another moment, huddled near the tail car on Armato's side. No less a personage than Nicky A. himself was crouching in the shadows there, a gunner Bolan took to be his number two beside him, covering.

All right.

He raised the rifle to his shoulder, sighting as his finger curled around the trigger and began to squeeze.

"ARE YOU a praying man?" Brognola asked the driver of the van.

"Not really, sir."

"Me, neither. I was thinking that it might be time to start."

The two black vans were rolling north on Broadway, drawing stares and glares from motorists as they kept pace with evening traffic. Branching off on Twentieth, they picked up speed, but Hal had nixed the use of lights or sirens. They were coming in on schedule, and he still had hopes of taking the combatants by surprise.

The battle would be joined by now, and someone at the yard would certainly have punched 911. Hal wondered if the locals would abide by their agreement to refrain from interfering or if someone at the cop house would be rolling out a riot squad.

It was a gamble, talking to the chief at all. Some members of his force were on the pad, as sure as hell, and reason told Brognola that Scimone and Nicky A. would both have eyes and ears in the department. It was only common sense, and why should Denver be the sole exception to a rule that seemingly applied from coast to coast?

The chief was straight, from what Brognola knew of him, but he would have to issue orders—to his deputies, to some dispatchers at the very least—and there was leak potential all along the line. If someone tipped off one or both of the contestant factions, Bolan's party just might be the washout of the season.

What was it the hippie posters used to say? He remembered it now: Suppose they gave a war, and nobody came?

Brognola put his own twist on the slogan. What if Bolan threw a party for the Mob, and no one showed? How would they ever find Carboni if the scheduled clash between Armato and Scimone was scrubbed for nonattendance?

They were three blocks from the rail yards when Brognola heard the gunfire, and he knew the meet was on. Whatever else might happen in the next few minutes, with Carboni and the rest of it, Hal understood that he would have his hands full.

Bolan would be on his own. Again.

Brognola raised the walkie-talkie to his face. "You ready, Leo?"

"As I'll ever be."

"It sounds like New Year's Eve up here."

"Or Independence Day."

"I'll see you on the ground, guy."

"Right."

At fifty yards Brognola saw the yard employees clustered by the open gates. They wanted no part of the heavy action that was going down inside, and Hal could hardly blame them. Given any choice at all, he would have been curled up beside his wife in bed, or maybe watching football on the tube.

But who had choices, anyway?

The burly Fed had cast his vote when he put on a badge, and once again when he had taken Bolan's hand in friendship. Some decisions canceled others out, and going back to simpler times was something you could only dream about.

His driver tapped the horn and scattered several stragglers as their van breezed through the open gate. Brognola's knuckles whitened as he gripped the Colt Commando carbine, double-checking to be certain that he had the safety off. Behind him, in the mirror on his right, he saw their backup hanging close as they began their run across the yard.

The firing echoed in his ears now as they swept past buildings on their left, a line of boxcars on the right. He couldn't see the action yet, but they were close enough for Hal to catch a whiff of gunsmoke.

"Let 'em know we're here," he ordered, and his driver keyed a switch to activate the lights and siren. Leo's van chimed in a beat behind the leader, and their strobes were flashing as they neared the battleground, both drivers standing on the brakes before they went too far.

It looked like hell. A couple of the limousines were burning, and he saw at least two railroad cars demolished on the sidelines. There were bodies everywhere, some deathly still, while others flopped and wriggled on the pavement. There was no time for a count just now, as Hal could see at least two dozen gunners trading fire across the open ground between their cars.

Some of them were distracted as the vans arrived with sirens wailing, and a number of the closest hardmen turned their guns in Hal's direction, laying down a spotty cover fire and caring not at all that they were firing on a group of Feds. A bullet cracked the windshield as Brognola disembarked, his carbine spitting out a short burst in response.

The shit was in the fan, all right, and Hal was wishing he had worn his waders as he looked for cover, breaking toward some kind of toolshed on his right.

And where was Striker—in the middle of the shit storm?

Taking care of business, right.

It was the only way to go.

ONE MOMENT, Joe Lolordo had a pistol in his hand and he was shouting at the troops to move their sorry asses, then a bullet struck him in the face and he was down, his blood and brains all over Nicky's suit. It took a heartbeat for Armato's mind to register the fact of Joey's death, and then he felt his stomach rolling, threatening to bring his dinner back before he got a grip.

So many of his boys were dead already that one more hardly mattered in the scheme of things. But this was Joey, damn it, and the suit cost seven hundred dollars if it cost a dime. He wasn't sure about the blood and brains, but Nicky knew damn well there wasn't any laundry in the world that could remove the smell of death that filled his nostrils.

"Kill those fuckers!" He was ranting at his soldiers now, his anger mounting to a fever pitch. "What is it with you guys?"

But Nicky knew exactly what it was. They were outnumbered, stunned by the explosive charges Patsy must have rigged before they got there, and their numbers had been damn near cut in half by hostile fire.

He stopped his feverish thought. No . . . that was crazy. If Scimone had rigged the charges, why had some of *his* troops been demolished when the boxcar blew? And what about the blast that took out Patsy's limo, seconds after one of Nicky's cars went boom? Armato's people didn't have that kind of hardware with them, and it didn't make a goddamn bit of sense . . . unless it was the wild card!

Nicky's mind was reeling as he tried to understand what had befallen him. Who *was* the wild card, anyway? Was it Omega, or the fabled Vince Carboni? Was it Mack the Bastard, after all? And did it make a difference while their lives were riding on the line?

Armato had two cars in working order, and he meant to save himself while there was time. It didn't take a fucking prodigy to realize that they were losing here, and if he stuck around a few more minutes, Nicky would be just another number in the nightly news report. It wouldn't matter, then, who pulled the trigger. Dead was dead, no matter how you tried to dress it up and hide the bitter truth.

He duck-walked toward the tail car, reached the driver's door and pulled it open, sliding in behind the wheel. The dome light flared for just a second, but he closed the door again and darkness settled in around him, broken by the muzzle-flashes of a couple of dozen automatic weapons.

Reaching out for the ignition keys, Armato found them in their proper place and cracked a little smile of pure relief. The simple pleasures, Jesus. Nicky almost flooded it the first time he turned the key, but the engine caught and he was rolling, shifting down into reverse. A couple of gunners nearest to the limo caught his move and tried to come on board, but Nicky wasn't in a mood to wait around. They had another car to use if they were game enough to try, and every second wasted put him that much closer to the grave.

He whipped the steering wheel around and grimaced as he clipped one of his buttons with the off-side fender. Stupid bastard should have watched where he was going, anyway. Armato made a more-or-less complete one-eight, pointing back in the direction he had come from—what? ten minutes earlier?—and floored the gas.

The instantaneous reaction was a killer.

Nicky never saw the high-explosive round in flight, and there was no way he could brace himself for the explosion as it hit the limo's trunk and blew on impact. He was barely conscious of the shock wave that immediately thrust him forward, seat and all, against the dashboard, snapping off the steering wheel, the jagged column plunging through his chest. In something like a half a second, well before Armato's wasted life had time to flash before his eyes, the fuel tank detonated in a secondary blast that turned him into smoking charcoal where he sat.

If anybody mourned the would-be capo's passing, they were too damn busy at the moment for their grief to show.

SCIMONE HAD SEEN the Feds arrive, and as a veteran of the violent streets, he knew when he was beaten. Once a couple of his boys had tried to match the new arrivals, going down before the guns, Pasquale figured he could run or take his chances with the courts. One option placed his life in jeopardy; the other had him looking at a prison term. But if he kept his mouth shut like a stand-up guy, the lawyers would be made available, and he would still have something waiting for him when he finished off his time.

Some choice.

At least he *had* a choice, and that was more than he could say for any of the boys he saw spread out around him, lying in their own blood on the pavement. For a "peace talk," it was anything but peaceful in the rail yard, and it struck him funny that the cops had only sent two vans. A mess like this should probably have called out half the black-and-whites in town.

Unless the cops *weren't* cops!

It was a classic ruse, and it had been perfected in his own hometown, when Scarface had dressed his gunners up like cops to fox the Bugs Moran gang back in 1929. Some Valentine's surprise that massacre had been, but Patsy wasn't falling for the ruse himself. Armato must be crazy if he thought that scam would work on wiseguys from Chicago.

Leaning close to Rocco Fanelli, Patsy yelled, "those guys ain't cops!"

"Say what?"

Before he could explain it to his second in command, Scimone watched Rocco die, a bullet ripping through his neck from left to right and taking out the jugular along with the carotid artery. The heavy hitter looked surprised, and then he just looked empty as his body toppled backward, melting in a boneless sprawl.''

"Those guys ain't cops!" Scimone declared to anyone who might be listening. He made a grab for Rocco's weapon—Fanelli wouldn't need it now, for damn sure—making sure the safety was released before he swung the little submachine gun up and fired a burst in the direction of the bogus Feds.

They dressed like cops—he had to give them that. A fucking SWAT team at a glance, but where was all their mandatory backup if they were legitimate?

"You can't fox me, you bastards!"

Patsy staggered to his feet, still firing, breaking for the cover of some boxcars on his left. If he could reach the shadows there and lose himself while they were mopping up his boys, there still might be a chance. If he was only quick enough...

The rifle shot that killed Scimone was a precision piece of work, delivered from behind him and above. The 5.56 mm round impacted at the base of Patsy's skull and clipped his spine as neatly as a scalpel might have done, exploding from a ragged exit wound beneath his chin. The nearly headless corpse remained erect for several heartbeats, then collapsed, the life run out of him like sand escaping from a broken hourglass.

CARBONI LIFTED OFF the AUG as Patsy fell and shifted his position slightly, tracking back toward Bolan. He had watched the soldier make his run, marked time when Bolan disappeared behind the railroad cars directly opposite and waited for his prey to reappear. He knew that Bolan was not running from the fight. The wily bastard was merely securing a better vantage point.

Carboni had the vantage point he wanted, as it was.

He perched atop a sort of warehouse-cum-garage with a commanding view of everything that happened down below. From the beginning of the carnage, he had followed Bolan's strategy, aware that no one else could possibly have orchestrated the fiasco being played out on that stage. His "brothers" from Chicago and Los Angeles had clearly come prepared for war, but they had also come to talk. The high-explosive charges and the rest of it were Bolan's work, a masterstroke to light the fuse and let short tempers do the rest.

Carboni didn't mind at all, nor was he worried by the late arrival of the Feds. They couldn't interfere with him when he was this close to his goal. One shot was all he needed. One clean shot, and Bolan would be his.

He had abandoned plans of meeting Bolan face-to-face when he had seen the layout of the chess board, realizing that a confrontation in the midst of so much chaos would be suicide. It was enough for him to kill the soldier now, let Bolan die with the humiliating knowledge of his failure to retrieve the woman.

Not the end that Vince had hoped for his most lethal enemy, but it would have to do.

He spotted Bolan between two boxcars, and he raised the AUG, stock snug against his shoulder as he sighted down the barrel. Filling up his lungs, Carboni let a portion of the breath escape, then swallowed hard to lock the rest inside. His hands were steady as Mt. Rushmore when he squeezed the trigger, gently, gently, careful not to jerk it as he fired.

And in the final fraction of a second, Bolan moved.

Carboni blamed it on the gunner from Chicago, who had caught sight of Bolan in the shadows and was rushing toward him, firing wildly with a 12-gauge, driving Bolan back and under cover. Vincent's round was wasted, flattening against the boxcar's metal side, and with a bitter curse he dropped the muzzle of the AUG, his finger tensing as he pumped off three quick rounds to drop the stupid gunner in his tracks.

"Take that, you fucking moron."

When he raised his sights again, the Executioner was back—and staring right at Vince. Their weapons fired together, with Carboni knowing he had blown it as a string of tumblers from the M-16 came sizzling in above his head.

"God *damn* it!"

Scrambling backward, Vincent reached the ladder that had brought him to the roof, descending in a rush that nearly made him lose his footing twice.

The bastard would be after him, no doubt about it. There was no percentage in a face-off here, with Feds already mopping up the dregs and tagging toes. Carboni's best chance was escape—or the *appearance* of escape.

If Bolan followed him, so much the better. Maybe they could have their one-on-one in spite of everything. The woman might be useful, after all.

Why not?

Carboni started for his car but took his time.

He didn't want to lose his shadow on the way.

THE BURST OF RIFLE FIRE that spared Mack Bolan the necessity of killing one more gunner also told him that Carboni had arrived. How long the sniper had been watching, Bolan neither knew nor cared. It was enough to see him on the roof some sixty yards away, with firelight from the battlefield reflected on his shiny, crinkled face.

The next burst out of Bolan's M-16 was meant to pin his adversary down without inflicting mortal damage. If he killed Carboni now, Val's whereabouts might never be revealed. He needed one more conversation with the scar-faced psychopath, just long enough to pry the vital piece of information from his shriveled lips.

It seemed a long run back along the line of railroad cars and around the far end of the killing field, with stray rounds snapping at his heels. He didn't pause to answer any of the LA. gunners, knowing they would have their hands full with Brognola's SWAT team in another moment, concentrating on the sprint to reach Carboni's hiding place.

The rogue Ace would have scrambled clear by now, of course, but something in his heart told Bolan that Carboni would not travel far. Their fates were intertwined, at least in Vincent's twisted fantasies, and if Carboni shook him now, who knew when they might meet again?

The guy would wait because he had no choice. Carboni wanted Bolan badly enough to sell his soul, and that was all the edge that Bolan needed now.

He reached the corrugated metal building, worked his way around in back and ducked a 3-round burst as he emerged from cover, catching sight of Vince Carboni on the move. Before he had a chance to try and wing the runner, Vince was gone, a nimble shadow dodging out of sight behind another building, leading Bolan toward the wire perimeter and parking lot beyond.

So be it.

Bolan followed, weaving as he ran and snapping home a brand-new magazine into the M-16's receiver. There was no point going up against Carboni with a partial load when every round would count and one could make the crucial difference in survival.

He was there. A hasty glance around the corner, and he saw Carboni dodging through the open gate, escaping toward a car parked on the street. The soldier's wheels were farther, but he had no option as Carboni made the car and slipped behind the wheel, the taillights flaring like a pair of ruby eyes. A burst at this range was as likely to decapitate the driver as disable the machine, and Bolan couldn't take the risk.

He sprinted for his car and got there moments later, diving in and fumbling with the key before he got it right. The engine came to life beneath his hands, and he was reaching for the brake when he beheld Carboni waiting for him at the far end of the block.

Of course. The crazy bastard wanted him to follow—*needed* it, in fact. It was the reason he had kidnapped Val, the reason they were all in Denver playing games of life and death.

"You got it, pal," the Executioner announced through gritted teeth before he pressed the Chrysler's pedal to the floor.

20

Carboni kept the headlights in his rear-view mirror as he traveled north on Wynkoop, twice avoiding a collision by the narrowest of margins as slower vehicles blundered out of driveways into his path. He didn't bother with the horn, preferring to amaze them as he whipped around each obstacle with screeching tires, the chase car slowing, swerving, never losing contact.

Vincent hoped that Bolan was a decent driver. Otherwise he might be forced to double back and find the bastard, which would make it rather obvious that he was setting up a trap. He didn't think a warning would deter the Executioner by any means, but there was no point taking chances.

At the safehouse, everything had been prepared. The woman was secure inside her cell, perhaps the worse for wear, but still alive and more or less intact. She would be ready when the trap was sprung, and she could watch her one-time lover fry before the flames consumed her own frail body, inch by screaming inch.

Carboni's face was flushed as he began to fantasize about the scene. He almost felt the heat, a wicked combination of his memory and keen imagination, picturing Mack Bolan as he stumbled through the burning house, half-blind and choking on the smoke, his crisp flesh peeling from his bones. The woman was dessert.

Carboni made the left-hand turn on Nineteenth, running east, and slowed his pace until the lights of his pursuer fell in place behind him. Traffic on the larger street had nearly taken Bolan out. Vince made a mental note to watch it on the next few turns and keep his prey in sight.

It was a classic setup, Bolan charging to the rescue, eager for the kill, with no idea that *he* would be the victim of the moment. To be fair, the odds were good that he had recognized the suck by now, but he was following Carboni, anyway, which meant that he was thinking with his heart and balls instead of with his brain.

Carboni caught a right on Blake and headed north with Bolan riding in his shadow all the way. So far, so good.

His preparation of the house had taken time, but he had done some work before he grabbed the woman, more while she was still unconscious from the chloroform. The task had been completed just that afternoon, while Vince was still keyed up from their encounter, one-on-one. False modesty aside, it was a masterpiece.

He had positioned cans of gasoline throughout the old two-story house—in closets, underneath the stairs, in various abandoned rooms—where they would add a little extra boost when things got rolling. For the main event, a propane tank had been connected to the structure's ventilating system. When Vincent turned the valve, its contents would begin to flow along the ducts from room to room, the heady fumes expanding as they displaced oxygen, the house becoming no more than a giant crematorium just waiting for the spark.

Carboni would provide that spark himself once Bolan was inside the trap. Of course, his human prey would quickly recognize the danger; the fumes would be enough to tip Carboni's hand. Once Bolan was inside, however, he wouldn't retreat without the woman. Chivalry was his abiding weakness, and it was about to cost the Executioner his life.

Carboni's own escape routes had been planned with care, the memories of fire and agony sufficient to encourage a fastidious approach. He had concealed extinguishers at half a dozen crucial points throughout the tinderbox to help him if he was cut off from doors or windows. Likewise, several ladders made of rope were hidden near the windows in the rooms upstairs in case his early moves with Bolan led him that way.

West on Thirty-eighth, and they were getting closer now. Carboni thought that he could almost smell the smoke.

Ideally he would spend some time with Bolan first before he lit the soldier's funeral pyre. In dreams and waking fantasies, Carboni always had a chance to tell the bastard who he was and why he sought revenge. The Executioner would have to be disabled—knee-capped, possibly, or wounded in the spine—to guarantee a good slow burn, but that wasn't a problem for a marksman of Carboni's caliber.

The woman was his hole card. He would show her to his quarry, let the soldier feast his eyes, before the trap slammed shut. It was a risky business, toying with a desperate man who had not been disarmed, but caution and precision were Carboni's watchwords.

Show the woman first, tell Bolan why he was about to die—it would be asking too damn much for Bolan to remember him or recognize his face—and fire before the bastard had a chance to think. If necessary, settle for a flesh wound, anything to slow him down and block return fire while a second, more effective round was placed at some strategic point, eliminating any possibility that Bolan could escape.

From there it would be Vincent's choice to kill the woman outright, Bolan watching, or disable her and let her fry. He thought it would be sweet—almost romantic—for the two of them to die together, black and crispy in each other's arms.

The problem was, that only happened in the movies. From his own experience, Carboni knew it was impossible to stand your ground and face the flames without a whimper. When the fat was in the fire—your *own* fat, anyway—there wasn't any time for lover's vows or holding hands like Jack and Jill.

From Thirty-eighth, Carboni made a right-hand turn on Brighton Boulevard with Bolan trailing as they traveled northbound under Highway 70. Beyond the underpass, the names changed, Brighton turning briefly into Williams and as swiftly back to Brighton, stockyards fast approaching on his left. Carboni powered through another turn to make the side street, losing sight of Bolan for the first time as the house came into view.

He needed time enough to grab the bait and arm the trap before his prey intruded. Two, three minutes ought to do it if he kept his wits about it.

It was all the time Carboni needed.

It was all the time that Bolan had.

VAL HEARD THE CAR pull up outside, the engine cutting out, and she began to tremble. It infuriated her, this fear that she could not control, but images of her attacker and the brutal pain he had inflicted crowded out her conscious efforts to be brave. She clutched the tattered nightgown close around her body, vowing to herself that she would die this time—or make him kill her, yes—before she let him savage her again.

She felt unclean, despite the fact that she had showered twice in nearly scalding water, trying to erase the vile sensation of his hands and body on her flesh. She thought of Jack at once, and cringed inside as she imagined his reaction to the news of rape. He would be strong, of course, and say the right, supportive things, but Val would always wonder what was going on inside his mind. The articles in women's magazines depicted lives and marriages destroyed by sexual assault, the wounded husband feeling guilty for a failure to protect his woman, wondering—as all men wonder, so the authors said—if maybe she was "asking for it" somehow, even secretly enjoyed the brutal treatment. Jack was not like that of course, and yet—

Val hesitated, knowing it was foolish to concern herself with what might happen in the days to come. The way things stood, she had no future. There was every chance that she would die inside this house, within these very rooms. Perhaps today—or was it night? And did it matter when or where a person died?

Damn right, it mattered.

When the scar-faced bastard came for Val this time, she would not make it easy for him. She had learned from her mistake, the kick that he had parried with disastrous results. This time, when he was close enough for Val to reach his eyes, she would repay him for the pain he had inflicted in their last encounter. If he killed her in the process . . . well, at least it would be better than another rape.

She heard his footsteps in the hall outside, and she retreated to the farthest corner of the room. There would be no way she could hold her shredded nightgown closed and use her hands for fighting all at once, but modesty meant nothing to her now. The animal had seen her, *used* her, and her first concern was paying back some measure of the hurt—both physical and mental—that she had endured.

He stopped outside her door, a key scraped in the lock and Val was ready when the door swung open to reveal her captor standing on the threshold with a pistol in his hand.

"Come over here," he said. "I need your help with something."

Val refrained from goading him with angry words, but neither did she move. Her rapist crossed the room in long, swift strides, and Val was ready when he came in range, her lunge planned out in every detail, visualized before she made the move.

It didn't help.

The burned man caught her with a short punch below the solar plexus, doubling her over, and he cracked the gun across her unprotected skull with force enough to split her scalp. Val felt the warm blood on her neck, behind her ears, as she collapsed on hands and knees before him. She was gasping, cursing breathlessly, when he drew one arm back behind her, fastening the cuffs, securing her other arm with easy, economic moves.

He dragged Val to her feet before she caught her breath. Her legs felt like spaghetti as he shoved her through the open door, then along the hall in the direction of some stairs. She felt humiliated, helpless and exposed. Her big resistance number was an abject failure, and the bastard had her at his mercy once again.

"Your boyfriend's on the way," he told her, grinning with his thin, discolored lips. "We're going to surprise him, you and I. A little party for the hero and his girl."

She stumbled on the stairs deliberately, but her abductor used the cuffs to haul her upright, putting pressure on her arms until she thought they would be twisted from their sockets. Tears of pain and anger painted tracks across her cheeks.

Upstairs he prodded her in the direction of what seemed to be a linen closet. When the door was opened, Val saw empty shelves on one side with a stationary ladder mounted on the other wall.

"Inside," he ordered, shoving her ahead of him when she appeared to hesitate.

Above them in the ceiling of the closet was a trapdoor hinged to open upward. It would serve the attic, Val decided, or at least a crawl space underneath the roof.

"This won't take long," he said. "Why don't you have a seat?"

Without a hint of warning, Val's abductor hit her with a forearm smash between the eyes. She crumpled in a corner, dazed and hurting, on the verge of blacking out. When she could see again, with objects more or less in proper focus, he was climbing backward down the ladder, with the trap still open overhead.

"All set," he told her, reaching down to grab her hair and drag her upright. On his clothing, in the very air around them, Val smelled propane.

She tried to speak, and got it right the second time around.

"What are you doing?"

"Putting on the final touches for our little celebration," he informed her. "What's a party, anyway, without the fireworks?"

Moving back along the upstairs corridor, she still smelled propane. The fumes were everywhere, it seemed. A sudden flash of insight made her struggle to escape his grasp, but he responded with a sharp jerk on the handcuffs, burying the muzzle of his automatic in her ear.

"Don't give me any crap," he snarled. "You've served your purpose, as it is. I'd like to let you see the guest of honor one more time, but if you fuck around with me, I'll kill you where you stand. That clear?"

She didn't answer, and he gave the gun another painful twist.

"That clear?"

"It's clear."

"Okay, that's better. Why don't you and I just take a stroll downstairs and see if anybody wants to join the party."

This time, when she stumbled on the stairs, it was an accident. He caught her, clinging to the handcuff chain, and Val could not suppress a painful cry as both her arms were levered back and upward. She no longer thought about the nightgown, open like a flimsy robe in front. The pain—her knowledge of the searing, agonizing death to come—was everything.

What happened in a fire? Val made a conscious effort to remember everything she knew about the subject, sorting out her thoughts and separating fact from fiction. The majority of victims died from breathing smoke and other fumes, she understood, and they were dead before the flames attacked their flesh. There was a bit of sage advice, delivered by medieval executioners to victims facing immolation at the stake, and she had heard the words repeated by a fireman friend of Jack's some years ago.

Then the thoughts, filtered into her shocked mind. If you were ever *really* trapped by fire, without a prospect of escape or rescue, face directly toward the flames and breathe as deeply as you could. With any luck, the heat would sear your throat and lungs, producing swift unconsciousness and death before you had a chance to burn alive.

"This way."

He prodded her along the corridor until they reached a sparsely furnished living room. There was a ratty sofa in the middle of the room, a coffee table just in front of it. Val sat where she was ordered to, and her abductor settled in beside her, one arm draped across her shoulders while the other pressed his automatic to her side. His glassy eyes seemed distant, thankfully unconscious of her nakedness beneath the open gown. The smell of propane was growing stronger all the time.

"He won't be long," the gunman told her. "I imagine he's outside already, but he won't take any chances with the door. That gives us time. I've got a story you should hear."

THROUGH THE CHASE, Mack Bolan hoped Carboni would be leading him to Val, preparing for a replay of the showdown that had left him scarred, inside and out. If she was dead, then he could pull out all the stops, but first he had to know.

On Brighton Boulevard he passed the Denver Union Stockyards, with a cemetery up ahead. His quarry turned before they got there, Bolan trailing through the turn and nearly losing him so close to home. He overshot the house but glimpsed Carboni's Chevy from the corner of his eye and doubled back to park obliquely on the far side of the street.

It was an old two-story house and might have passed for an abandoned hulk without the car parked in the drive. The homes on either side were certainly unoccupied, their windows dark and vacant like a dead man's eyes.

A perfect setting, Bolan thought. No neighbors to ask questions or report suspicious movements, no one to disturb with screams or gunshots if it came to that.

Was Val inside?

The Executioner knew only one way to find out.

He left the Uzi and the M-16 behind, relying on his side arms as he left the car and crossed the street. Carboni might be watching from the windows—he would certainly be ready, waiting—but the Ace could not be everywhere at once. If Bolan kept him moving, guessing, there was still a hope of penetrating his defenses, getting close enough to score a kill.

It would have helped to know how long Carboni had been planning and preparing for this night. The house might well be booby-trapped, inside and out, for all that Bolan knew. If Val was here and still alive, a rash attempt at rescue might result in sudden death—and yet, what options did he have?

He circled past the carport, pausing long enough to slice the valve stems off the two rear tires. Carboni would be going nowhere fast in that machine, no matter what went down inside, and Bolan turned his full attention toward the penetration of the house.

No doors, for starters, front or back. If Vince was laying snares, the doors would be his first line of defense, rigged up with anything from trap guns or explosives to electric current channeled through the knobs. If nothing else, he could defend a door by simply waiting on the other side and sniping anyone who entered as they stood in silhouette against the night.

A window was the way to go. He ruled out entry through the kitchen or the sitting room in front because of close proximity to doors. The rest were likewise unappealing, curtains drawn and locks in place. It would take time and noise to breach the ground-floor windows, and he would be vulnerable if he started climbing to the second floor.

He found his answer on the west side of the house when he had nearly finished off his circuit of the premises. A basement window, thick with grime and more or less forgotten, tucked away behind a wall of prickly weeds that overran the flower beds. He tried the window, found it latched and spent a moment working with the Ka-Bar, opening the rusty catch with nothing more than minor squeaks and scrapes.

It was no time for hesitation. He wriggled through head-first, the brush of spider webs against his face producing goose bumps. He imagined something crawling down the collar of his skinsuit, but he let it go, refusing to alert Carboni with the sound of slapping at an insect. Black widows and the recluse spider were the only ones of any consequence, and neither of them worried Bolan at the moment, with a more pernicious enemy in front of him.

The basement was apparently secure. His penlight found the workbench with its tools, a block and tackle hanging in the middle of the claustrophobic room, a recent bloodstain on the concrete floor below. His stomach churned when Bolan thought of Val, suspended from the hook and screaming out the final seconds of her life, until he forced the image out of mind and concentrated on the stairs.

He killed the penlight halfway up, relying on a slit of light beneath the door. If it was locked, then he would have to try Plan B, a smash-and-enter ploy that might surprise Carboni or allow him time to drop the hammer on his guest. But then why would Carboni lock the basement door if he had overlooked the window leading to the yard?

One way to know for sure.

He drew the Desert Eagle, thumbing back the hammer as he climbed the final steps, his lifetime boiling down to what transpired within the next few seconds. Reaching for the knob, he tried it, felt it turning in his hand. No shots and no explosion, no alarm bells as he cracked the door and pulled it toward him, inch by inch.

The room beyond was lighted by a ceiling fixture, two dim bulbs without a globe, but it seemed bright to Bolan's eyes. He spent a moment on the threshold, making the adjustment, listening for any sound that would betray the presence of his enemy. Before he took two steps, he recognized the sour, pervasive smell of propane that seemed to come from nowhere and from everywhere at once. He couldn't place the source, and yet—

At first he thought the sound of voices—no, one voice— was actually his own pulse beating in his ears. It took a moment for his mind to pick out syllables and words, still unintelligible from a distance but distinctly human.

It was not Val's voice.

He moved in the direction of the sound and froze immediately when the droning stopped. He waited in the hallway, scarcely breathing, pinned between the pantry and the parlor just ahead.

"We've been expecting you," Carboni said, a note of tension in his voice. "Why don't you join us?"

Bolan did as he was told, the Desert Eagle leveled at his waist. His first view of the parlor showed him Val—alive, thank God—with Vince Carboni standing just behind her, one arm wrapped around her neck, the one complete hand he possessed rock-steady with an automatic pistol pressed against her cheek. Val's nightgown was ripped open in the front, from neck to hem, and she was naked underneath.

The setup had been calculated as a blow to Bolan's senses, but it had the opposite effect. In place of shock or fury, he felt grim determination, cold as ice behind his eyes and inside his chest. The Magnum automatic in his right hand never wavered from his target. One twitch on the trigger and 240 grains of screaming death would rip through Val, between her jutting breasts, to nail Carboni where he lived.

It was a perfect shot that Bolan knew he couldn't take.

"I was afraid I lost you," said his enemy, the crinkled face convulsed in something like a smile. "It would have been a shame."

"I'm here," the soldier said. "Let's play."

"We are. It's started."

"You don't need the woman, Vince. It's one-on-one, the way you wanted it."

"Don't tell me what I want!" Carboni's eyes were blazing now. "You haven't got the first idea of what goes on inside my head."

"I think I do. You tried for me in Baltimore and blew it. Rather than admit your failure, you've been working on a story that would make it all my fault. You want revenge, and now I'm here. What are you waiting for?"

"Who's waiting? I've already made my move."

The stench of propane was stronger now, and Bolan glanced in the direction of a ceiling vent.

"I see you've turned your hand to home improvements," Bolan said.

"You like it? Just a little something I dreamed up for central heating. It should keep you nice and toasty on a night like this."

"You wouldn't care to join me?"

"Thanks, but no. I've been that route, and this one's all for you. I only wish that there was someway I could make you feel what happens *after*, if your luck runs out and you survive."

"You still don't need the woman, Vince."

"*You* need her, though. I thought you might."

"Why hide behind a skirt, Carboni? Aren't you man enough to face me on your own?"

Carboni sneered. "Let's ask the bitch what kind of man I am. She's had a sample, and she loved it. Didn't you?"

The last two words had been addressed to Val, and Vincent gave her head a twist to make her gasp in pain. In that split second, when his eyes and his attention were diverted from their proper target, Bolan made his move.

It was a deadly risk, but there might never be another chance to strike. He brought the Desert Eagle up in one swift motion, squeezing off a thunderclap almost before his eyes had time to sight along the slide. It was a brash, instinctive shot, and if he missed the mark by so much as an inch, the boattail slug would rip Val's face in half.

Instead it clipped Carboni's elbow, shattering the joint on impact, spinning him around and pushing him away from Val before he had a chance to scream. He kept on going, using the momentum of his spin to take him out of Bolan's range, an awkward, headlong dive across the sofa, disappearing with a crash.

Deprived of her support, Val staggered sideways, lurching, dropping to her knees. Without a hand to catch herself, she toppled forward on her face, her forehead making solid contact with the floor.

A glance showed Bolan that somehow Carboni had retained his weapon. Whether he could use it was another question, but they had no time to wait and see. He darted forward, slid an arm around Val's waist and lifted her, retreating toward the door that led outside. When they were halfway there, he swiveled toward the ceiling vent and triggered off another round at point-blank range.

His muzzle-flash ignited something in the air duct, and he heard a mighty whoosh as flames caught hold inside there, racing backward to their source. He wrestled Val around the corner as a tongue of flame lapped downward through the vent and caught the carpeting below. A second vent, behind the couch where Vince Carboni had concealed himself, was also drooling fire.

They reached the porch as flames began to flicker in the upstairs windows. Then Bolan was hauling Val across the weedy lawn. Behind them, in the attic, something blew with force enough to lift a section of the roof, expelling shingles bright with flame like luminescent autumn leaves.

He knelt with Val and held her tightly as they watched it burn. The screams were muffled for an instant, small and far away, until Carboni's body cannonballed through glass and screen to strike the porch, a leaping scarecrow etched in flame. His voice was like an echo out of hell, and Val pressed both hands tightly to her ears.

Mack Bolan raised the Desert Eagle, bracing it in both hands, sighting on the spastic figure as Carboni reached the steps and started toward them, leaving fiery footsteps on the lawn. He emptied out the magazine in rapid-fire when one round would have done the job, dispatching unearned mercy to a tortured soul.

Except it wasn't mercy.

It was making sure.

EPILOGUE

The waiting room at Booth Memorial's emergency division would have been deserted but for three men seated in the corner farthest from the nurse's desk. The two on either side wore suits and ties that had been hastily acquired, by all appearances. Their faces registered fatigue. Between them, taller than the others, sat a man whose face was smudged with soot, his jacket covering a skintight turtleneck that reeked of propane.

From time to time the three men spoke among themselves, but mostly they were silent. They ignored the television, where a manic talk-show host was flirting with his leggy guest and calling for a film clip from her latest cinematic farce. The men in waiting seemed to have no interest in the world outside of their immediate surroundings, waiting for a verdict on the patient whom the tall man had delivered thirty minutes earlier.

"She'll be okay," Brognola said for something like the fifteenth time since he'd arrived. "You said yourself she looked like she was holding up."

"We'll see," the Executioner replied.

At Bolan's left hand, Leo Turrin cleared his throat to speak. "We missed Armato and Scimone," he said. "I mean, we *got* them, but we didn't bring them in alive. Their boys are sitting in the county lockup, waiting for their lawyers . . . those who made it, anyway."

"I got Armato," Bolan said. "Carboni got Scimone."

"Carboni?"

"It was half of why he came, remember? He was punishing the Families, too, for throwing him away."

"At least we've seen the last of him," Brognola said. "The crazy bastard won't be coming back this time."

"*We*'ve seen the last of him," the Executioner agreed. "I couldn't say the same for Val."

"She'll be—" Brognola caught himself. "Well, Jesus, she's alive. I mean with Jack and everything, she'll put it all together. She's got guts she hasn't even used yet."

"Maybe."

"Maybe, hell. You ought to know her well enough to see she'll bounce right back from this. When Harold the Skipper had her up in Boston—"

"This is different," Bolan interrupted.

"Well..."

They hadn't talked about the rape in any detail, and they never would. Brognola had an inkling of the trauma Val had undergone, and he was wise enough to know that no man *really* understands unless he's spent a night in jail with cellmates who had lust on their minds.

"Is there a Mr. Blanski here?"

The doctor had surprised them, slipping up behind the nurses' desk.

"I'm Blanski," Bolan said, impressed that Val had thought to use his code name in the circumstances.

"We're admitting Mrs. Gray for observation, and she's been sedated, but she'd like to see you for a moment."

"Right."

The doctor led him through a set of swinging doors that had no locks or knobs. Outside the treatment room, he turned to Bolan, pausing.

"In a case like this, we normally expect the next of kin."

"Her son is flying in on the red-eye. We expect him sometime in the next few hours."

"And I understand that you're a special friend?"

"We've known each other for a while."

"I see. The patient has survived an ordeal which she's only hinted at, to me. All things considered, she's in decent shape. I see no obstacles to physical recovery, but her mental state . . . you understand?''

"I won't upset her," Bolan promised him.

"There is a sense of guilt—entirely undeserved—in cases such as this. I thought that you should be prepared."

"Okay."

"Five minutes, now. No more."

The room was bright enough to hurt his eyes, and Val seemed almost radiant in starched white gown, a sheet pulled up beneath her arms, with snow-white pillows underneath her head and shoulders.

"Hi," she said.

"The same to you."

"You saved my life . . . again."

"You've got a life worth saving," Bolan told her. "Johnny's on his way, and they tell me Jack's all right. He'll need someone to help him get around until he gets the crutch-and-cane routine down pat."

The tears came suddenly, without a hint of warning, and she pulled him close, her fingers closing on his arms like claws.

"Oh, Mack . . ."

He kissed her lightly on the forehead, pulling back enough that he could look her in the eye.

"You don't have anything to be ashamed of, Val. What happened, happened. It was never your idea, and there was nothing you could do to stop it."

"Jack—"

"Has brains enough to recognize the truth. You think that he'd stop loving you if you were bitten by a snake?"

"Of course not, but—"

"That's all it was. The snake's dead, Val. You may catch glimpses of him in your dreams, but he can't hurt you anymore."

"I had a lot of time to think when I was locked up in that room. I thought about a lot of things."

"Such as?"

"The way I let John fill you in about my wedding plans. All kinds of things. I let you down."

"I think you've got that backwards, Val. You saved my life in Pittsfield and you gave the kid a home when all that I could think about was looking out for number one. This is the second time I almost got you killed. We both know who's responsible."

"I should have waited."

"Are you happy?"

"What? With Jack?"

"That's what I mean."

Her eyes went misty then, and Bolan read the answer for himself before she spoke.

"I love him dearly, but it's not the same."

"Thank God for that. You have a man there every day to help you through the rough spots. I'm no good to anyone around the house."

"It's not your fault."

"Okay, let's say you're right. That doesn't make it yours. The plain fact is, you've given me a reason not to quit. I owe you more than I can ever say, much less pay back."

"We sound like a mutual admiration society."

"That's not so bad. It's hard, sometimes, to find a person worth admiring."

"I've got three," she said.

"And two of them can't wait to see you on your feet again."

"The third?"

"He's history."

"I wish—"

"Don't say it, Val. There's truth in what they say about not going home again."

"I was about to say I wish that you could come and visit us in Sheridan someday. Of course, we'd have to sneak you in and hide you in the attic, I suppose."

He grinned and held her hand, old lovers and forever friends.

"I might," he said. "You never know. I might, at that."

"Okay, then. It's a date."

"First chance I get."

"I'm awfully sleepy."

"It's the medicine. I'll let you get some rest."

"Don't go until I fall asleep. You promise?"

"Cross my heart."

"And hope to die."

"Not yet," he told her, and repeated it for emphasis. "Not yet."

ABLE TEAM ®
DICK STIVERS

Check out the action in two ABLE TEAM books you won't find in stores anywhere!

Don't miss out on these two riveting adventures of ABLE TEAM, the relentless three-man power squad:

DEATH HUNT—Able Team #50 $2.95 ☐
The lives of 20 million people are at stake as Able Team plays
hide-and-seek with a warped games master.

SKINWALKER—Able Team #51 $2.95 ☐
A legendary Alaskan werewolf has an appetite for local Eskimos
fighting a proposed offshore drilling operation.

Total Amount	$ _____
Plus 75¢ Postage	.75
Payment enclosed	$ _____

GOLD EAGLE ®

ATD-1

TAKE 'EM NOW

FOLDING SUNGLASSES
FROM GOLD EAGLE

Mean up your act with these tough, street-smart shades. Practical, too, because they fold 3 times into a handy, zip-up polyurethane pouch that fits neatly into your pocket. Rugged metal frame. Scratch-resistant acrylic lenses. Best of all, they can be yours for only $6.99.

MAIL YOUR ORDER TODAY.

Send your name, address, and zip code, along with a check or money order for just $6.99 + .75¢ for delivery (for a total of $7.74) payable to Gold Eagle Reader Service.
(New York residents please add applicable sales tax.)

Remove from pouch...

unfold once...

unfold twice..

and they're ready to wear.

GOLD
EAGLE

Gold Eagle Reader Service
3010 Walden Avenue
P.O. Box 1396
Buffalo, N.Y. 14240-1396

GES-1AR

Offer not available in Canada.

Do you know a real hero?

At Gold Eagle Books we know that heroes are not just fictional. Everyday someone somewhere is performing a selfless task, risking his or her own life without expectation of reward.

Gold Eagle would like to recognize America's local heroes by publishing their stories. If you know a true to life hero (that person might even be you) we'd like to hear about him or her. In 150-200 words tell us about a heroic deed you witnessed or experienced. Once a month, we'll select a local hero and award him or her with national recognition by printing his or her story on the inside back cover of THE EXECUTIONER series, and the ABLE TEAM, PHOENIX FORCE and/or VIETNAM: GROUND ZERO series.

Send your name, address, zip or postal code, along with your story of 150-200 words (and a photograph of the hero if possible), and mail to:

LOCAL HEROES AWARD
Gold Eagle Books
225 Duncan Mill Road
Don Mills, Ontario
M3B 3K9
Canada